FOREVER LINKED

Lori Bell

Copyright © 2016 by Lori Bell

Cover photograph by CanStockPhoto

http://www.makemoneyinlife.com/websites-to-sell-art-online.html
https://www.fbi.gov/about-us/investigate/vc_majorthefts/arttheft/national-stolen-art-file
http://www.artloss.com/about-us
http://www.biography.com/people/william-jennings-bryan-9229920#synopsis
http://www.cancercenter.com/leukemia/symptoms/?source=MSNPPC&channel=paid+search&c=paid+search%3ABing%3ANon+Brand%3AExact%3ANon+Brand%3ECancer+Type%3A+Leukemia%3AExact&k_clickid=7ecfec2f-2e1c-14c8-1a72-0000274e04a2

Printed by CreateSpace

ISBN 978-1523709632

DEDICATION

To my daughter, Bailey. I look at you and I see a little of myself and a lot of your father. You are an extraordinary twelve year old, and I know one day you will be an amazing woman. While I wish I could have kept you little, in my arms and on my lap, I know time must march on. My greatest wish for you is the obvious. Find love. Be happy. Stay healthy. And then there is my hope for you. I hope with all of my heart for you to find your passion. Never give up when there is something you want to do, or be. Dreams do come true.

Chapter 1

It was the moment she had been dreading for the past forty-eight hours. The devastating truth was still rippling through her body. Her heart and her soul were broken. And now, to see her friend, lifeless, was entirely too much for Sax Arynn to handle.

Life was like that. People took for granted there would always be another day. But then, in an instant, anything could happen to change a path. Change a heart. Or break a heart.

Sax felt shaky in her two and half inch heels. Her straight black pencil skirt reached her ankles, where she had a chain-link anklet inked on her skin above her left foot. She was alone in the funeral parlor. The family would be there soon, the funeral director had told her when he allowed her some time alone. The hours were going to be limited now. The clock was ticking on how long the face of her friend would be visible on this earth. It was a frozen, at rest, lifeless face. But still, it was her. It was a chance for Sax, and everyone else who would file past this open casket in the next two days, to see Jenner Wibbs one last time.

Sax was relieved to be alone when she reached the side of the coffin and she let out a whimper before covering her mouth with her hand. She briefly and tightly closed her eyes as tears instantly seeped and streamed down her face. Her ash brown hair was cut short, a few generous inches above the back of her neckline, and worn longer and full on the top where it was parted wildly and unevenly chic on one side, leaving her long bangs to partially cover her right eye.

"This isn't how it's supposed to be. Not how it's supposed to end, Jenner." Sax's words were barely a whisper, but she was speaking outright and alone in that room which could have felt creepy if she had let it. Just her and a dead body. But, it wasn't like that. This was Jenner, her closest confidant in the world. Not even death could separate them. Sax wondered if that were true. *Would Jenner always be with her in spirit? Would lights flicker or significant scents seep through the air, to alert her that Jenner was there? And how could that ever be enough compared to truly having her there?* It wouldn't.

Right now, all Sax could think about was sadness. Sobbing. Touching her hands, her cold, stiff hands. Fixing a hair out of place on her head. Her poker straight blonde hair reached her shoulders and Sax smoothed out a few loose hairs near her eyebrows and she followed one long strand on down to her collarbone.

"You look damn good, considering," Sax told her, as she thought about when she heard the news. The mature police officer wasn't very gentle with his word choice when he said Jenner had wrapped her car around a tree. A car accident claimed her life at merely thirty-three years old. Sax only saw a few scratches on her, not really deep enough to describe as cuts, which makeup did not entirely conceal. One was above her eyebrow and another below her chin. She was wearing a blue cowl neck sweater. That color always made her eyes pop, Sax remembered. *If only she could open her eyes. One more time.*

∗ ∗ ∗

Hours passed and Sax stayed near the back wall of the funeral parlor. She was in the same room as the family, friends, and the endless line of people coming in to pay their respects. She wasn't in the receiving line to hug, talk to, and cry with anyone, but she was there. She was present to witness the pain in people's eyes and the sad aura that lingered in the room. Even from clear across that room, Sax couldn't keep her eyes off of the body in the casket pushed up against the front wall. That body was her best friend. That body was a corpse. Jenner was dead, and Sax was sure she would reel from this loss for the rest of her life.

* * *

Sax sat at her kitchen table. It was one of those tall rectangular shaped vintage wooden tables with high-back chairs painted sea green. There was silence in her kitchen. The uncomfortable kind where Sax felt as if she should be talking, asking questions maybe just to fill the air. But, as she looked across the tabletop at twelve-year-old Quinn with her nose in a science textbook, she chose to just leave it be. Her long, thick, wavy, blonde locks reached far down her back. Sax smiled as she focused on the scattered freckles across the bridge of her nose. Those freckles were from her father. And so was the natural wave in her hair. Everything else was her mother's. Her blue eyes. Her infectious, wide smile. Jenner loved her daughter with her entire being. And now that love was missing from this child's life. The mere thought of it, and my how Sax could over think it, sickened her.

An abrupt knock at the front door of her yellow house on the corner of Dietrich Street interrupted Sax's thoughts as Quinn closed her textbook and said, "My dad's here." Sax stood up from the table in unison with Quinn as she reminded her to grab her backpack propped up against the wall behind her.

"How long do I have to stay with him this time?" Quinn asked her, and Sax tried to appear like she believed Quinn spending time with Zane Ski was a good thing.

"Just a few days, but I'm here anytime if–"

"If I need you," Quinn interrupted with a tone that could have easily been accompanied by an eye roll. "I know. Thanks. But what I need is my mom and we all know that's not happening. Sucks knowing I have a lifetime ahead without her." This was the most open Quinn had been with Sax since Jenner died just three weeks ago. She had been stoic and nonchalant about everything. Sax was concerned, but giving her time. It was still too fresh. Too raw. And the shock remained. They were interrupted by a second, louder knock at the door.

"Oh," Sax spoke, momentarily forgetting he was there. "Do you want me to ask him to give us a few minutes? To talk?" Quinn shrugged her shoulders and Sax decided to take that as a yes from a preteen who didn't always communicate well.

Sax quickened her steps toward the door and flung it open. "Zane, hi. Come in, but could you give us a minute in the kitchen?" Sax was looking at a six-foot-two, scrawny-framed man with wavy shoulder-length light brown hair. He was wearing faded black jeans with high laced black boots. It was cold outside but he was only wearing a white t-shirt, untucked, and his tattooed forearms could have been mistaken as sleeves. Sax wasn't even sure what all that ink symbolized. She never did ask, and she didn't want to stare. Zane nodded his head and Sax told him he could wait in the living room. "Would you like a drink? Soda? Water?" She refrained from offering him a beer as he was about to drive with his daughter.

"Don't make me feel at home," was his reply and Sax forced her face to remain expressionless. He could come across as an ass, Jenner used to say, but his appearance and tough persona were only a cover. Sax understood. She made strong look invincible. She had been through more hell than most people knew, but that's what gave her beauty an edge.

Sax made her way back into the kitchen and found Quinn zipping up her backpack, now on the chair. "I know you're in pain, crazy pain. I'm right there with you. We can talk about it...if you want?" Sax felt like holding her breath as she took a few steps closer to Quinn, but stopped when she looked away from her and down at her backpack.

"My dad is waiting," she responded.

"He'll give us a few minutes if you want to talk..."

"Maybe some other time," Quinn was quick to answer as she slung her backpack over her right shoulder.

"Okay, sure," was all Sax responded, trying not to sound disappointed or impatient.

Sax followed her to the doorway and then Quinn stopped and turned back around. "Sax?"

"Yes?" Sax asked her, nearly startled by how much this young girl could often sound exactly like her mother.

"Will you call me tomorrow?" Quinn asked.

"You know I will," Sax responded, moving in for a quick, tight hug as she whispered, "love you" into Quinn's ear. And, *see ya*, was all she heard back.

Sax watched them leave as she stared out of her living room picture window. It was an old house, but a fixer-upper was what Sax had wanted five years ago when she moved in. New windows were on her to-do list still, as she noted feeling how drafty that particular window could be on a cold, winter's night in Salem, Illinois. With her hand, she brushed the hair away from shielding her right eye as she noticed how the two did not act like father and daughter. Quinn trailed a few steps behind Zane as they made their way to his 1984 white Mustang. Once they settled inside the car and drove off, Sax finally stepped away from the window. She walked over to turn on the lamp in the middle of the sofa table which sat up against the full length of the back of the pale yellow sofa. Yellow, dull not bright, was her favorite color. The lamp flickered while Sax still had her hand underneath it. She stared at it, and watched it flicker again.

Sax smiled, a crooked grin which symbolized being unimpressed with what was happening before her very eyes. "You're going to have to do better than that, Jenner," Sax spoke aloud and outright in her empty living room. And then all the lights, including the TV, on the main level of her house went out. Only for a few seconds though. Just long enough for Sax to get the message. Jenner was there. She was with her. And she would see her through this crazy pain.

Chapter 2

Sax stuck the needle into the easily visible vein and filled two vials with blood. She firmly pressed a ball of cotton in the bend of the middle-aged woman's arm and then wrapped and tightened a dressing around it. She told the woman to *have a nice day* as she exited the patient room adjacent to the hospital lab.

Sax had been a medical technologist at Salem Hospital for her entire career, which was eight years thus far. That's where she met Jenner. Jenner worked as the Director of Nursing at that same hospital.

She could still remember the day she saw her in passing, in one of the hospital corridors. Both of them made eye contact at the same time, smiled sincerely, and greeted each other. One more meeting just like that led to conversation and then lunch in the cafeteria. They wholeheartedly agreed later how there were times when people met and instantly felt like asking, *Have we met before?* There's a connection. A bond. A level of comfort that only exists between friends. That was Sax and Jenner six years ago.

Sax made her way to the outdoor courtyard, still wearing her white lab coat in the brisk forty-five degree air. She reached deep into her pocket and pulled out a loose cigarette and her lighter. She lit up and inhaled what felt more and more like her lifeline.

"That shit will kill you," a voice from behind spoke to Sax, and she turned around and purposely blew smoke, long and forceful, from her mouth in the direction of Rue Bray's face. Rue was thirty-something years older than Sax, and as her supervisor she felt it was also her duty to mother her. Rue's upper body fat giggled as she fanned away the smoke in the air near her. "Well, you ornery cuss," she said with a crooked smile and Sax returned one to her.

"How are you doing, honey?" Rue asked, worried about her. She could see right through her tough exterior, but Sax didn't let many people in. Jenner was one of the lucky ones. Jenner was such a huge part of Sax's world, and losing her was devastating. But, Sax never let that show. Never let her guard down. Not even to Rue. Not yet anyway, but she was working on her. She had an annoying tendency to stick her nose in everybody's business.

"I'm fine," Sax replied, finishing the rest of her cigarette and this time she politely turned her head to exhale the smoke.

"How's Quinn?" Rue continued to press.

"She's doing okay. She's a strong little girl," Sax replied as Rue watched her lit eyes. It was so obvious how much she cared for Jenner's daughter. A child she had met six years ago and grown to love and care for as her own. Sax turned away from Rue as the wind picked up and her short cropped ash brown hair covered more of her right eye than usual.

"I'm sure you're there for her if she wants to talk," Rue began again, "just as there are people in your life who are here for you. Myself, included." Sax nodded her head and muttered, *thanks*. But, she didn't mean it. She wasn't grateful for *people in her life* who claimed to have *a shoulder for her to cry* on or to be there *to catch her when she falls*. She could cry just the same all alone in her house. And, if she felt like hitting rock bottom, well, she would do that alone too.

"Pretend I'm Jenner," Rue said, attempting to pull up the collar of her lab coat around her bare neck, but the coat was entirely too tight to even budge an inch on her short, stocky, apple frame.

"What?" Sax asked, feeling a cross between unnerved and humored. No one could touch Jenner Wibbs. She was a tall, thick but shapely built, blonde beauty with flawless skin, perfect white teeth and piercing blue eyes. So the idea of pretending the graying, past the point of chubby woman standing before her, was Jenner, was comical.

"Open up to me like you did with her," Rue told her.

"What are you now, a counselor?" Sax replied, sarcastically.

"No. I'm only someone who sees what losing your best friend is doing to you. You can't hide it, and you certainly can't get by for too long bottling up those feelings. Emotions like that will eat you alive." Rue planned to say more, but that's when Sax turned and walked away. She escaped before Rue could see the tears welling up in her eyes. What Rue did see when she looked down at her feet on the ground was Sax's cigarette butt. It didn't appear to be completely extinguished. There was still some smoke seeping from it. Just like Sax, she thought. There was still life left within her. Her spirit wasn't completely out.

✳ ✳ ✳

The cruise control of her charcoal gray metallic Dodge Challenger was set on sixty in a fifty-five speed zone on the drive home from work. Sax passed the spot, the exact location of that dreaded tree planted deep in its roots just slightly off-road, which she never wanted to see again, but it was on her well-beaten path every single day. She remembered again the police officer's words. Jenner had lost control of her car, and *wrapped it around a tree.* There were no guardrails or concrete barriers to prevent cars from veering off the roadside. Jenner's vehicle had gone airborne and came into direct contact with that fat, oak tree sitting entirely too close to the road. Now, it was the tree's fault.

The toxicology report had shown that Jenner's blood alcohol level was three times the legal limit. They never should have agreed to share that second pitcher of margaritas at the Mexico on Main restaurant. Sax should have taken Jenner's car keys. But, she was intoxicated too. They were tipsy, not drunk. That's what they had said to each other, and themselves. It's what they did. This wasn't the first time and *who the hell knew it would be the last?* Instead of thinking or dwelling or making a big deal out of their alcohol consumption when their girls' night ended a little out of hand, Sax hugged Jenner close and tight in the parking lot where their cars were parked adjacent to each other, and then she drove one direction and Jenner took off the opposite way.

Sax remembered setting the air vents on the dash in front of her on high speed. It wasn't warm outside, maybe in the forty-degree range, but the air conditioner was on cold and blowing directly on her face. To keep her awake, to sober her up. *Eyes on the road. Watch your speed. All you need is for a police officer to pull you over and issue a DUI. Or, for an accident to happen.*

Now, Sax pulled into the driveway of her yellow house on the corner of Dietrich Street, and sat behind the steering wheel after she turned off the engine and sighed. The feelings of grief and loss and sadness consumed her. *Would any of it ever completely go away?* She doubted it would, because she knew the friendship she shared with Jenner was unlike any other. She would love and miss her for the rest of her life.

Six and a half years ago, just before Sax and Jenner met, Sax's life as she knew it for three years was over. The love of her life, Seth Moss walked out on her. They were going to get married, or so Sax had believed. He loved her, or so he had said. A job offer in Chicago was an answered prayer, a dream come true. For him. He was moving and Sax had said she would too. Finding a job as a medical tech at a hospital or clinic wouldn't be too difficult. She was even willing to just get a job and put her career on hold. For him.

But he said he needed to do this alone. Move. Launch a career in computers. Start a new life. Sax was shocked and heartbroken. She obviously was the one with the greater need. She had loved him, and trusted and believed in them more than he ever had.

She mourned him and their relationship for days that turned into weeks, months, and then years. She still carried so much pain in her heart. Jenner had told her time and again to allow those wounds to heal over and turn to scars if need be. But, just let go.

Jenner's friendship, love, encouragement, and unwavering support had gotten Sax over the hurdles. Was she past the point of raw pain? Yes. But, not a day passed where she didn't think of him. Sometimes with hatred. And many times still with love. She couldn't shake the incredible love she had felt deep inside of her heart for a man who didn't want her, afterall.

There were times when she still saw him. In a crowd. Driving a car, in passing. Close-shaved ash brown hair, just like the color of hers. It was never really him though. But her heart fluttered and her cheeks flushed as if it were when she saw someone else with a momentary uncanny resemblance to his five-nine muscular frame that began with broad shoulders and a thick chest.

With the car engine turned off, Sax was beginning to feel chilled still sitting behind the wheel in her single-car garage. She picked up her handbag off of the passenger seat and her cell phone out of the cup holder between the seats. She got out of the car, slammed the door with a push from her rear end, and walked inside of the house. She entered the kitchen first and slipped out of her two-inch black heels as her wide-legged black dress pants now dragged on the beige-tiled flooring. Her fitted silvery turtleneck sweater felt cozy against her skin in the kitchen that always kept a cooler temperature than the rest of the house. Probably because the windows, the corner two above the sink and the other near her high dining table, were the draftiest in the whole house.

Immediately after Sax took off her dress clothes, she slipped into a black half-zip athletic pullover and gray sweatpants. She never liked the elastic around the leg ends. It was an old style that had come back around in fashion. With this particular pair she had taken a scissors to the ends to remove the elastic and to loosen and flare the legs around her ankles. It was her favorite, most comfortable pair.

Sax plopped down on the end of her pale yellow sofa with her cell phone in hand. She had been busy all day at the hospital while Quinn was in school, but now would be a good time to call, she hoped, as she waited for her to answer.

"Hi Sax," Quinn said after three rings. She sounded upbeat.

"Hello Quinnster, how was school today?"

"Okay," she replied, because she was an honor student and did enjoy socializing with her closest friends.

"Am I interrupting homework?" Sax asked, hoping she wasn't because she wanted to talk to her for awhile. It had been three days since she last saw her and the past two days they had only texted.

"No. I finished already," Sax replied.

"So what are you doing now?" Sax asked, keeping their conversation going.

"Waiting for *him* to get done painting so we can eat dinner." Zane Ski was an artist through and through. His art studio was housed in his home and there were days and nights that ran together for him as he painted the hours away. He easily would forget to eat, which explained how thin he was, and his lack of sleep often shown on his face. His life was his art, and some still liked to call him *Salem's starving artist*. Zane wasn't a wealthy man, and probably never would be. But, occasionally, one of his pieces sold well enough online which allowed him to live, or get by, without having to get a real job. He wasn't acclaimed across the country, but a few of his paintings hung in museums in St. Louis.

Jenner loved art museums and she had spent a great deal of her spare time browsing them. Late one night she had been alone and strolling through her favorite contemporary art museum in downtown St. Louis when she crossed paths with Zane. They had nothing in common except for art. She loved it. He created it. And their one night stand had created Quinn.

"Have you ever shared your drawings with your dad?" Sax asked, knowing this girl had a rare, raw talent already as a preteen.

"No!" Quinn was quick to answer, adamantly.

"Why not? Your work is phenomenal. Your mom raved about it, and I've seen for myself!" Sax never wanted to stop mentioning Jenner to Quinn. She wanted to keep her alive in their everyday conversation. She could share so much with Quinn because she and Jenner had been in each other's lives for half of Quinn's life. Memories were made. Stories were told. Sax needed to share all of that equally as much as Quinn needed to know it, absorb it, and retain those memories as treasures.

"He's not interested in my art, or me," Quinn spoke with certainty, not sadness. "We both know if my mom had not died, I would still be living a very separate life from this man who I'm now supposed to call *dad*, and live with. Jesus Christ, Sax. He's a stranger to me. I don't even have his last name. Mom used to say I'm a Wibbs through and through."

"Except for your freckle bridge..." Sax began.

"And the waves in my hair...." Quinn added, with a smile in her voice.

"Otherwise, you are your beautiful mother," Sax spoke, swallowing hard the lump that wanted to surface in her throat and pierce tears in her eyes.

"Through and through," Quinn responded.

Chapter 3

Seth Moss walked out of the high-rise building in the City of Chicago and hailed a taxi cab. He threw his briefcase on the seat before he got inside and told the familiar cabbie to take him home. As the cab sped off parallel to the clustered traffic, Seth stretched his legs a bit and put both of his hands behind his head. His elbows were pointed outward as he momentarily closed his eyes and thought about what he had just said. Take me home. *Home.* He had never felt like he was home, there in Chicago.

It's been six years and seven months and he had yet to feel like the Windy City was meant to be for him. His job as an Information Security Analyst, for which he specialized in protecting companies and their data from hackers, was all he had hoped it would be, and more. He worked in cyber defense to keep the hackers out, as well as in forensics where he implemented the reverse-engineering attacks to figure out who was stealing data and how. Seth's career was exciting nonetheless. But, his life outside of his career didn't fulfill him. He had friends and occasional women to date, but those women were just warm, sexy bodies. He had yet to meet a woman who made him feel like Sax Arynn. A woman, two hundred and fifty-seven miles away, whom he was well aware he had abandoned with a broken heart. There were no two sides to that story. He was wrong. And he knew it. He was consumed with regret, but he believed it was too damn late now. She would never forgive him or accept him back into her life ever again. And, besides, a woman like her more than likely had a new life, a new love. Seth wanted that for her. He truly did.

✳ ✳ ✳

Sax was sound asleep on the pale yellow sofa in her living room. The TV was on with the volume low, and she was covered up to her chin with a white afghan. She was in the midst of a dream where she could see him so clearly, sitting somewhere with his arms up, hands behind his head, and a smile on his face. That wide smile used to melt her heart. Now, the thought of it, even in a dream, only broke her heart.

The next morning, Sax never remembered that dream but she did awake on the couch feeling heavy-hearted. As she got herself ready for another work day, she sent Quinn a text before school. *How about dinner tonight?*

A few minutes later, Quinn responded. *Okay.* And then Sax told her, *Pick you up on my way home from work. 5 ish. We will eat out. Your choice.*

Two smiley faces then came across Sax's phone screen and she knew this was going to be a good day. If Quinn was happy, so was she.

It was five-fifteen when Sax parked her vehicle alongside the street in front of Zane's house. He had a short, narrow rock driveway, but his outdated white Mustang already occupied that space. His tiny house, with white siding that could have used a thorough power wash, sat in the middle of Salem's business district. There was a bakery on one side of the house and the post office on the other. That mix of business and residential zoning had never made sense to Sax, she thought while she walked up the cracked, uneven concrete sidewalk and made her way to the front door. Quinn had not come out to meet her, so Sax was preparing to knock and go inside.

After one knock, the door flung open and Zane was standing on the opposite side. "Hi," he said first. "Come in." Sax smiled politely and stepped up one step inside. She was immediately standing behind one brown floral sofa, facing another with an ugly green plaid pattern only about ten feet directly in front of it. The living room was terribly cramped and the furniture, the carpet, and everything else was tattered and old. He still had a tube television set, which was on and blaring loudly in the far left corner of the small room.

"Is Quinn ready?" Sax asked noticing Zane was wearing his trademark washed-out black jeans, calf-high black boots, and a white short-sleeved t-shirt. This shirt had paint splattered all down the front of it.

"Almost, she'll be right out," Zane responded. "Thanks for making plans with her tonight. She's happier when you're around."

Well then let me have her, Sax thought to herself before she spoke. If only Jenner would have prepared for the worst and had a will drawn up. Sax would have raised that girl in a heartbeat. Instead, she was stuck living in a rundown shack with her biological father. A man she barely knew. "We need to work together to make her happy more often," Sax chose her words carefully.

"Sure," was his response and Sax noticed again how he seemed different. Happier, she guessed. And then she wondered why, or what had changed? Maybe having his daughter living there was good for him, afterall. If so, Sax wanted it to be good for Quinn, too. She was all that mattered to her.

Before Sax could once again bring up the possibility of hiring an attorney to sit down with them and formulate a shared custody agreement in which they could compromise on, Quinn bounced through the open doorway between the kitchen and living room, wearing her backpack on both shoulders and a smile on her freckled face. "I'm ready!" she said, and Sax assumed she still had homework left to do, and she didn't mind helping her. But first, they were going to eat dinner.

"Wonderful," Sax said, opening her arms to a hug that Quinn initiated. "What's on the menu for us tonight?"

"No pizza, I've had it all week. I need a meal with vegetables, please." Quinn was serious and Sax looked at Zane.

"What twelve year old begs to eat veggies?" Sax asked, trying to hide her disapproval of Zane and everything about him.

"No kid of mine. I haven't eaten a vegetable since I was forced to by my mother. And what the hell is wrong with pizza anyway?" Zane asked his daughter, wanting to add that she was *as weird as her mother*, but thought twice and knew he shouldn't.

Quinn rolled her eyes at both him and his question as she started walking toward the front door. "Don't look for me early. I'm doing my homework at Sax's house." There, Sax had her answer and they had a plan for the evening. A well-balanced dinner and homework. Most importantly, they would have time together.

✶ ✶ ✶

During dinner, Sax watched Quinn eat a garden salad smothered with Ranch dressing, followed by two pieces of fried chicken, mashed potatoes with gravy, and a cooked mixed vegetable medley of carrots, peas, and corn. Sax had all of the same on the plates in front of her, but she didn't eat half as much as Quinn. It was like eating with Jenner all over again. That woman never wasted food. Quinn's frame was still that of a preteen, but Sax could see her one day being tall, and thick but shapely, like her mother. Jenner had been built like a movie star from the nineties, and that was why Sax used to lovingly call her *a blonde Julia Roberts*. Sax, on the other hand, was a few inches shorter and curvier as a size six. She could never eat as much as a Wibbs girl, not without paying for it in her jeans. Her personal trainer always reminded her to never eat until she felt full. More frequent, smaller meals, was what he preached.

"So your dad seemed cheery tonight," Sax said, bringing up what was still on her mind. "Does that mean things are better? Or at least going well?"

"He sold some of his artwork online this week, and it must've been for a good price because he was able to pay off some bills and I overheard him on the phone, making plans to transfer some money into a new account at the bank." Quinn seemed unaffected relaying this news to Sax, but Sax was intrigued.

"Well that's wonderful for him," and she was going to say *and for Quinn too*, but Quinn had her mother's inheritance money. She would be okay, even supported through her college years. Still, maybe Zane making a decent amount of money for a change could lead to a better lifestyle, starting with decent meals and maybe better living quarters, for both him and his daughter, Sax thought while she pushed her fork through the last of the mixed vegetables on her plate.

On the opposite end of town, Zane sat behind his computer. A laptop was placed on top of a card table in the corner of his art studio. His studio was a spare bedroom in his house that was completely empty, except for his office corner and a half a dozen easels placed where the carpet had been ripped up and paint-splattered floorboards remained.

He was intently searching a website he had stumbled upon only days ago. He felt like he had struck gold, and maybe he had. He'd known for fifteen years, or more, that if an artist places artwork anywhere on the Internet, there's a risk of getting it stolen. He, personally, always put a watermark on his paintings. That transparent marking with his Z-Ski logo gave him peace of mind. He knew of other artists in his circle who chose to inable the download of the artwork's full image online. But, Zane believed that if the buyer could not see the entire piece, it would not sell.

On the computer screen in front of him, Zane was scrolling through thirty-four paintings. An artist, by the name of J.Zimmer was new to the scene, or at least Zane had never spotted or heard of him, or her, before now. Forty-eight hours ago, Zane pulled an all-nighter in his studio, rushing and somewhat sprinting from his laptop to his easel, not even taking the time to set down his paint brush. There were trails of colors, all colors of paint, on the floor in a zigzagged path from the middle of the room to the far right corner. Two of J.Zimmer's paintings had caught his eye and he couldn't shake what he was feeling. Combined, he knew he could paint a masterpiece, or at least the best work of art he had ever created. And it didn't deter him, or worry him the least bit, to know it was not truly his creation. It was someone else's idea, and he stole it. And it was incredibly easy to take and run with it. It was not protected. The artist was obviously green. Or, maybe, just a believer in personal artwork being automatically copyrighted at the moment of its completion and protected from acts of infringement. Zane knew, according to the United States Copyright Law, how that was true. He also knew all artwork was not completely protected without further action. J.Zimmer had made a major league mistake, and Zane was acting fast so he could be the first person to infringe upon his work.

It had been a year and a half since Zane made any real money off his original artwork. He profited small sums, and he lived how he was used to living. Was he comfortable? Sometimes. And other times, he felt as he was known, as a *starving artist*. Zane's artwork was original and good. Damn good. He believed in himself. He just had not been able to tap into his imagination and really create as of late. He needed something or someone to inspire his creative juices. And, now, someone had. Another artist. The *work* of another artist.

He had painted a combination piece of someone else's two paintings. It was crazy how stunning the piece in front of him looked in the wee hours of the morning when he finally had stepped back, stared intently, and called it complete. By the next day, he downloaded that piece online with copyrights all his own. Usually, he would price and sell his pieces immediately. This time, he first chose to open it for bid. Within fifty-seven minutes, Zane had his first bidder. For one hundred thousand dollars.

He thought he was imagining the impossible at first. Surely, there was a mistake. He had never seen that kind of money for one painting alone. His work in fifteen years had not come close to even adding up to a total like that. He even accepted a considerable cut in profits to have two of his paintings on display in both museums in St. Louis. He convinced himself it was about getting out there, being seen. And he was right. Every dreamer begins putting more into a dream than receiving. Sometimes that will pay off in spades. This time, Zane was certain he was on his way. This was his big break. The money, those six figures he had never seen in one lump sum before, had already been deposited in his bank account. He had purposely gone to a second bank in Salem where he had never done business before and that's where he opened an account to hold his new earnings. And now, he was studying the computer screen in front of him in hopes of being inspired to combine two or more of the pieces to create again. He would push to keep selling the first painting, of course, but while this new, inexperienced, artist had not secured his paintings from being infringed upon, Zane Ski was taking full advantage.

Chapter 4

Zane was surprisingly compliant when Sax texted to inform him that Quinn had fallen asleep on the couch watching TV after dinner and completing her homework. In one extended text, Sax had promised to bring Quinn home early the next morning so she could shower and get ready for school. Zane never read more than the first two lines of that text. His response was only, *Fine*, and then he resumed crafting his paint brush onto the canvas propped up at a slant on the easel in front of him. This time, he was combining three of someone else's paintings to create one of his own.

* * *

When Sax walked Quinn up to the front porch of Zane's house, it was six o'clock in the morning and still dark outside. The house, from the outside, also looked dark. Sax watched Quinn turn the knob on the front door to find it unlocked. She walked into the house, and Sax followed. It's what she did. She looked out for this girl. She never dropped her off without seeing Zane was present. And, now, she wanted to do the same. The living room was dark and Sax turned on the first lamp she found, on a corner table centered between the two sofas facing each other. "Do you think your dad is still asleep?" Sax asked, not keeping her voice low. She wanted to wake him. If he wanted to be a father to Quinn, he needed to start acting like one. Sax was only giving him so much time, so many chances. She actually hoped he would fail. It would make her attempt to gain full custody so much easier.

"I'm just going to take a shower and get ready for school, so it's okay, you can go." Quinn didn't seem fazed by the idea that she could be alone in that house.

"Absolutely not," Sax responded, as she began to walk through the house. She opened a door and realized it was Quinn's bedroom. She shut that, and continued to the next room. Zane's bedroom was empty. The bed was unmade. Clothes were scattered all over the floor and she shut that door and moved to the last room in the hallway. Zane's art studio.

That room was bright. The main ceiling light, with a fan, was on and lit the entire room. It was definitely a colorful mess in there, but Sax liked it. It was cool, if nothing else. Easels set up all throughout the room, bare floorboards paint-splattered. And then in the corner, where there was a card table and only one folding chair, was Zane. The laptop computer was turned on and he was slouched in the chair with his legs straight out in front of him, with his arms folded across his chest, and his chin resting downward, nearly touching his collar bone. Sax assumed Zane had fallen asleep while working. Before Sax woke him, she started to look at the paintings he was working on. One, in particular, in the middle of the room, caught her eye. It was beautiful. A landscape like she had never seen before. The grass was tall, the barn in the background was ancient, almost dilapidated. A man was sitting on the ground with his back propped up against the old splintered wood on the side of the barn with pain in his eyes, as he stared away in the distance at a woman wearing a white, cotton dress, flowing in the wind. She had her back turned and appeared to be taking steps to walk away. *Possibly from him?* Sax was mesmerized as Quinn interrupted her thoughts when she spoke to her from the doorway.

"He doesn't like anyone to see the paintings before they are finished," Quinn said, as her voice carried and formed an echo in that hollow room and instantly Zane woke up with a start.

"Oh, hi," he spoke as he stood up, somewhat stiffly from that hard-back chair. "I'd rather not have anyone in here." He was serious as he rose to his feet, still wearing those calf-high black boots, washed-out black jeans, and the now unrecognizable white t-shirt covered in paint.

"I'm going in the shower," Quinn spoke, and then left the room.

Sax looked at Zane and then back at the empty doorway. "I'll call you later, there is something we need to discuss," was all she said as she abruptly left the room, but not without glancing one final time at the painting in the middle. It was absolutely striking to her.

Sax drove back home to get herself ready for work. She slipped off her gray sweatpants and left them on the bathroom floor as she turned on the water in the bathtub shower. She stretched the fitted long-sleeved white t-shirt over her head and threw it on the floor where her pants already were. She stood there for a moment, looking at herself in the mirror before it would steam up from the hot shower water. She was wearing a black sports bra and a pair of black boyshorts. She was fit and curvy. Her body showed some obvious muscle from her daily workouts with a personal trainer. She felt sexy as she stood there, looking at her body. Her short, cropped hair was a little messy from sleeping, but the way it always partially covered her right eye defined Sax. She was the kind of woman who had things to hide. Her feelings, for one, were never completely out there for the world to see. At least not anymore. Life had taken her for a rough ride, and she had gradually learned how it was easier to close off and to keep her distance rather than risk pain.

She moved her boyshorts off of her bottom and kicked them over to the clothes pile. Then she maneuvered her full breasts out of the sports bra. It had been a long damn time since she allowed a man to touch her. Seth Moss had ruined intimacy for her. He was the perfect lover. So attentive. Such a man in the way he moved, the way he touched, just in every way. In the last six years, Sax had sex with other men. But, that's all it was.

Just bodily pleasure. Nothing more. Nothing like how it used to feel with that *son of a bitch.*

And that is how her memories of him always ended. She could lose herself in thinking about him, about them. And then the anger would surface again. Even though she believed that pain was no longer raw, it still was.

Later, Sax was wearing fitted gray tweed pants, dark brown knee-high boots with a generous block heel, and the same dark brown cowl neck sweater. She left the house without wearing a coat again. She always kept a coat on the backseat of her car, just in case, but preferred not to wear one. As she drove off, en route to the hospital, she again thought of that painting in Zane's art studio. She wanted to see it again, if she could.

The woman in the painting looked familiar. Felt familiar. Her thick, but shapely frame in a white, cotton dress, was real. From the side, a view of her poker straight long, blonde hair had obstructed her facial features, from what Sax could remember anyway. The next time Sax picked up Quinn from the house she was going to see that painting again. She had to.

✳ ✳ ✳

It was three days later before Sax had plans to see Quinn again. Quinn offered to take the bus after school to a stop near Sax's house, but Sax insisted she would pick her up. Sax was on break, standing outside in the hospital courtyard, smoking a cigarette, when she received a text from Quinn, who she assumed was in school.

We moved. Would you like to pick me up at my dad's new house?

Sax's eyes widened and she wanted to call Quinn to talk about this surprising move, but she knew Quinn was not allowed to have her cell phone powered on inside any classroom at school, and she probably was sneaking it right now.

Are you kidding me? Yes, I want to see it. Send me the address please.

When Quinn's next text came through with the address, Sax immediately punched it into Google maps. The location was exactly where she had thought. On the east edge of Salem there once was a six-hundred acre farm with a thirteen-room, two-story red brick house. The house still remained. It was the childhood home of William Jennings Bryan in the late 1800s. Bryan grew up to become a liberal leader and speaker who ran unsuccessfully three times for the United States presidency.

That home, which until recently was owned by the City of Salem, had been the Bryan Birthplace Museum for decades. But, in recent years, since Sax was a child, it was closed and sat vacant. Occasionally, tourists would call ahead and the mayor would arrange for a tour. That type of interest was few and far between though. Sax remembered taking a field trip there in grade school. She found it boring then to view newspaper clippings, as well as a variety of awards that man had received. The boys in her class were wound up about a flatiron and fire tongs from his boyhood home. The teacher had mentioned how the furniture there belonged to Bryan's parents, including a bookcase, washstand, and a desk, which were all on display.

Sax also remembered seeing Bryan's Spanish American war uniform, along with a chair from his office in Washington, D.C..

As she thought about all of that, she lit up a second cigarette in the courtyard. It was cold out there, but the wind was still and her white lab coat gave her another layer over top her cowl neck sweater. She was confused why the city would sell the museum as a house again, and even more baffled as to how it fell into Zane Ski's hands.

Sax sped away from the hospital at the end of her work day. She was going to pick up Quinn for dinner and spend some time at her house afterward. But, now, she was going to seize the opportunity to take a look inside of Zane's mansion on the outskirts of town.

She parked alongside the street, and just inches from the curb in the grass was a rickety, wooden, three-panel fence around the front of the house. It looked as if it was originally built to keep horses caged. Sax found the entrance gate and the latch was broken so she just slightly pushed it open. She walked up the narrow path and could hear her own heels on the concrete. When she reached the front porch, she noticed the four white pillars had paint chipping off of them. The foundation beneath her feet felt solid, but looked so old. And she noticed the door bell was rusting when she pressed her finger on it.

A few seconds later, Quinn opened the door. "Some place, huh?" she asked, rolling her eyes, and Sax stepped inside.

"And, this place, is now your dad's?" Sax asked, frowning a bit, but she was quick to lose that expression as soon as she saw Zane in the immense front entrance area of the house. The ceilings were incredibly high, at least twenty feet, and there was a stairway which led to a balcony above them.

"Yes, it is," Zane spoke loudly and his voice carried in the room which contained no furniture yet. Sax wondered if he would bring in his two broken-down, ratty sofas from the other house. She hoped not. But, furnishing a home costs money, and Zane Ski didn't have money for lunch tomorrow, much less to own an old mansion turned museum on the outskirts of town. *Did he?* Sax wondered if his artwork had sold even better than Quinn had implied recently.

"You never said you were moving," Sax said to him as he stood near both her and Quinn. He was wearing his usual uniform of black jeans, boots, and a white t-shirt. This t-shirt looked clean.

"I'm moving," he replied mockingly, and Sax smirked. "No, Sax, I never said because I didn't know. It just happened. I had an opportunity to take a chance, and I took it. End of story. This is my new home." Sax was unnerved how everything was addressed by him as his. He never included his daughter. Sax was certain Quinn didn't mind moving from a shack to a manor, but, still, she knew Quinn did not want to live with him. Anywhere.

Sax wanted to inquire about so much more. She didn't know him well though, nor were they close enough for it to be appropriate to talk about finances. She had never even heard this place was for sale. She imagined the City of Salem not being willing to sell a piece of history for cheap. Sax chose to push her curiosity aside and focus on Quinn. "So, do you have a bedroom here yet?"

"She will in a few days. I've ordered her a new set," Zane said, with an unusual air of confidence in his voice. "In the meantime I was hoping she could crash with you?" Zane asked.

"Of course she can. She can stay as long as she wants." Sax and Quinn both knew that was a jab at Zane because his daughter did not *want* to live with him.

"I'll give you a call when your room is ready, kid," Zane said, beginning to back away from them. "Right now, I gotta go, my art studio is the first thing they are setting up right now."

They? Now he had people working for him? "Sounds exciting," Sax said to him, feeling uncomfortable. And downright suspicious.

Chapter 5

For the next two days and nights, it just felt right to have Quinn living with her. They knew when to give each other space, and how to make the most of their time spent together. Sax could read Quinn almost as well as she read her mother. Quinn was a preteen who could be quiet and moody at times, but lately Sax noticed she seemed happy when they were together, just as Zane had mentioned. That was Sax's goal now. She wanted to make Quinn feel at home and to try to keep a smile on her face. That was difficult sometimes, because they were both still in the thick of their grief.

Before Quinn was dismissed from school, Sax left the hospital early. She had been allowing Quinn to take the bus to her house after school and let herself in. She was alone in Sax's house for almost two hours before Sax returned home from work. Today, however, Sax wanted to run a few errands and then be at home when Quinn arrived. One of those stops was going to be Zane's new living quarters.

When she pulled up alongside of the street again, Sax noticed two large retail trucks. She assumed furniture was being delivered. Two men in jeans and red hoodies came from the house and climbed into the back of one of the trucks. She could see the front door was propped open and there seemed to be some activity inside. More workers, she guessed, still in disbelief that Zane now had money to burn.

Sax wasted no time getting out of her car, making her way up the walk and then inside of the house, as if she owned the place. No one paid any attention to her when she stepped inside, placing her heels on what looked like new, dark hardwood flooring. There was a painter in the living room, where the walls now looked freshly painted with a dark shade of beige. Sax just started walking, hoping she wouldn't run smack into Zane anywhere. She could always fabricate a story about Quinn, but it couldn't be too outrageous because they all knew Quinn didn't want much to do with Zane. When she was away from him, she never spoke of him unless Sax asked.

She made her way up the stairway, which curved around to a landing that led to the second floor. Sax walked along the balcony, looking down and still not seeing any sign of Zane on the main floor. She assumed the path she was following would lead her to the bedrooms, or maybe the art studio.

Standing at the end of a long hallway, all Sax could see was a bunch of closed doors. She started to walk, and then one-by-one she opened each door, looked inside, and then closed it again. Most of the rooms were empty and had a musty smell in the air. She did find one, which she assumed was going to be Quinn's bedroom. She saw a bed frame with the mattress still wrapped in plastic, a long dresser set up against the same side of the wall as the door, and a stand-alone oval shaped full-length mirror with wood trim. A price tag was still hanging on the dresser. For the entire set, Zane had paid twenty-five hundred dollars. It was all for Quinn. Sax was impressed that he wanted to buy her something so nice, but she was seriously worried about how he was going to afford all of it. It wasn't any of her business if his artwork was suddenly selling well. But, this was just so incredibly strange and out of the ordinary for Zane. Sax didn't trust him. If Quinn was going to be in his care most of the time, Sax needed to know she was safe.

"Jenner, is this legit?" Sax spoke outright and alone in that room with only her and the new furniture. "Come on, give me a sign. Why am I so worried about this? I'm snooping around here like I'm trying to solve a mystery, or save the fucking day, or something!"

There was silence. The same silence Sax walked into when she opened that door. She was a bit unnerved. It seemed when she asked Jenner to be there, to reach out, she never did.

Sax carried on with looking inside mostly empty rooms. On that floor, she never did find an art studio or anything worth a second look. As she made her way back toward the stairway, she heard the front door close. From the balcony, she could see out of the window, the painter making his way down the walk.

She could also see one of the large trucks outside was gone. She assumed that was the two men in red hoodies who delivered Quinn's bedroom furniture. By the looks of the empty room, Quinn also assumed she was now alone in the house. There was a basement, too, she knew, and she wondered if maybe that was where Zane had set up his art studio.

When her heels reached the main floor, she again stood on that dark hardwood and briefly admired how nice it looked. She glanced around the empty room and tried to imagine what type of furniture would soon fill it. Anything had to be better than two raggedy sofas, but she wondered anyway.

There was a fireplace against the far wall with a mantel that looked ancient. It certainly had some history to it, Sax was certain, and believed that was probably why Zane had kept it. Sax stood still at the foot of the stairs and her eyes moved slightly to the right of the fireplace mantel. And that's when she saw it. The painting. The one with the barn and the man propped up against it, looking at a woman just a short distance away. That woman. Sax wanted to get another look. She needed to. She knew that was why she came there today. She had been searching upstairs for Zane's art studio and *that painting*.

As she hurried over to it, she wondered why a painting had been hung already, against freshly-painted walls. It seemed senseless to her. She stepped close to the painting which was now set in a beautiful silver-beaded frame.

Again, Sax was taken aback by the beauty of one painting, one image that appeared to be speaking to her. And she didn't know why. The woman caught her eye again. That cotton dress. Her tall, thick, shapely body. *Oh dear Lord,* Sax gasped and put her hand to her mouth as tears immediately sprung to her eyes. It was Jenner. The woman in the painting depicted Jenner Wibbs. The artist had captured her every curve. Even the way she slightly tilted her head sometimes when she was speaking or just lost in thought. The artist was Zane. And Sax was moved. *Had he really known her? When had he paid that close attention to her?* He painted in detail that was so striking, and Sax couldn't help but wonder now if he loved her?

She stared at the woman in the painting who was supposed to be her best friend. And then her eyes followed across the canvas to the man looking at her with hurt in his eyes. *Possibly yearning for her?* She was within reach, but he had already lost her. That was evident in the painting, and now so crystal clear to Sax. Zane had been in love with the mother of his child. She was out of his reach. Out of his league. But that had not stopped him from feeling what he felt deep in his soul. Jenner had never known. If she had, she would have told Sax. If she had, she may have allowed him to be a part of their child's life. Instead, he never knew his daughter and his love for her mother was something he kept well-hidden for more than a dozen years. Sax wondered if that would have mattered to Jenner. She did not love Zane Ski. She had explained to Sax how their night of passion was just that. *Great sex which happened to conceive the true love of my life, my daughter.* Those were Jenner's words. Sax knew for certain Jenner had no idea Zane was in love with her. Sax had no clue either. Until now.

She thought about how it really no longer mattered if Zane was in love with Jenner. Jenner was gone. Zane would just be another person to grieve and miss her presence. It was sad, really, and Sax started to again feel like, if she allowed it, grief could swallow her up.

"What are you doing here?" Zane's voice asked, quickly and suddenly, from behind.

Sax spun around, feeling startled. But, Sax was a master at hiding her emotions. She brushed the hair away from her right eye with her hand. It was a nervous reaction, but no one knew that. "Oh, Zane, I was just admiring the painting, the only painting you have up in here," Sax began to explain.

"I can see that, but what brings you here? Is Quinn okay?" For a moment, Sax thought she heard concern in his voice. But, when she looked at his face, into his eyes, she saw nothing.

"She's fine. She's in school," Sax replied. "I just stopped by to see if you would open yourself up to meeting with me and a lawyer. We could work something out so Quinn can have–"

"That's seriously why you came here?" Zane interrupted. His long dishwater blond locks were in a low ponytail and his eyes pierced hers as she saw wrinkled lines form on his bare forehead. He only had freckles across the bridge of his nose. "How many times do I have to spell it out for you? She's mine. Jenner never allowed her in my life and by some fucking stroke of luck she never made arrangements to keep her out of my life if something were to unfortunately happen to her. Well, she died, and I am that child's biological father and I finally am going to take full advantage of my rights!" Zane raised his voice and Sax pretended to be pissed, but really she was relieved. He had fallen for her excuse for why she was trespassing in his home.

"Fuck off, Ski!" she spat at him. "You may wonder why I bother trying with you, but let me tell you something, that little girl means more to me than my own life. She is a part of my best friend, who I will spend the rest of my days missing like crazy. I will never stop trying my damndest to get you to either cooperate with me, or give her up entirely. You know you will. What's really in this for you?" Sax was pressing him. She had forgotten how just moments ago she was looking at a painting by an artist that truly and so obviously had a heart. It seemed utterly impossible now to think those two people were one in the same, because Zane Ski was not a compassionate man.

"You have her now for a few days. Enjoy that while it lasts. And, one more thing, don't you ever come snooping around here again, you know, to ask me to give up my daughter." Zane turned on his heels and Sax kept standing there. His words had shaken her a bit as she watched him walk away. His tall, lean body, with a long ponytail halfway down his back.

It was as if he had an innovative spring in his step. He walked more confidently, carried himself more freely. Sax had never before felt so uneasy around someone.

Chapter 6

By the following evening, Quinn was back with her father. Sax dropped her off at the historic mansion on the east edge of Salem, and walked her inside the house to be certain Zane was there. She and Zane exchanged very little small talk and even less eye contact. Zane focused on telling Quinn her room was ready upstairs and how he hoped she would like her new bedroom set. Sax was thinking how maybe he should have allowed her to choose her own furniture. Afterall, she was twelve years old and not a little girl anymore. She had an opinion, and a specific taste already. Quinn only shrugged her shoulders. She did not want to be living there, or anywhere, with him. She had pretty much shut down by the time Sax left, feeling helpless and heartbroken.

Sax parked her Dodge Challenger in the garage and immediately shut the single garage door. That action mirrored how she wanted to shut out the world. *Just leave me the hell alone! I've lost everything that ever mattered to me.*

Sax made her way into the kitchen, and then walked through the living room. She was wearing her favorite gray sweatpants with a fitted white t-shirt and a black sweatshirt jacket with the zipper all the way undone. She shuffled her feet in white socks across the hardwood floor as she felt weighted and sad and her grief was overwhelming again. She glanced at the front door to her house and noticed it was unlocked. She assumed Quinn had forgotten to lock it again after she had asked her to go outside and get the newspaper. Sax was still very old school about reading the morning news in print, in hand.

When she walked over to lock the door again, it hit her. That wave of *you are alone, you are never going to be able to raise Quinn. You are going to spend the rest of your life pining away for a man who didn't want you.* She turned around from the door, but her back was up against it. She started to slide down the closed door with her knees bent. The tears were burning in her eyes. Like fire. And then her anger surfaced.

"You have no fucking idea how much I hurt!" she directed her anger at God. Sax had never been a woman of great faith. She didn't pray much to a God she did believe in, but couldn't fully trust. She was grateful for the blessings in her life during the good times, when she was happy and things were going well. Like when she was with Seth. And when she and Jenner shared and nourished an amazing friendship. Sax had yet to learn, or realize, that God not answering all of her prayers, or ceasing her suffering from pain and grief, didn't mean God was not with her. She had not known that faith was based on both. During the unbearable times, like Sax was in the midst of right now, she didn't believe that God was there. She never felt Him right beside her, trying to help her through the pain. Sax didn't want Him to see her through. She didn't want to be seen through anything. She could handle it on her own.

She stopped herself from losing strength. She stood up again, on her own two feet, and took one step away from the door. She had been standing on a rectangular-shaped floor mat. That particular yellow mat which spelled *welcome* in cursive dark brown letters was a gift from Jenner. It was a house-warming gift when Sax moved into this house, the first home she ever owned. Jenner had seen her yellow sofa, known she was obsessed with the pale yellow shade, and insisted she have a matching floor mat. Sax stared at that mat before she bent down in anger and grabbed one corner of it with one hand and swiftly and abruptly spun in through the air and across the room, like a Frisbee. Before it landed, it met with extreme force the lamp on the table directly behind her sofa. The lamp crashed to the floor and glass shattered.

"I... don't... care... anymore!" Sax screamed those words which seemed endless to trail off. She felt as broken as the lamp. She started to cry now as her knees bent and met the hardwood floor where the welcome mat had been. She cried hard and she cried for awhile. That's what inevitably happened to her after she bottled up her emotions. She preferred to cry alone. Besides, she believed there really wasn't anyone left in her life anymore for her to lean on.

Her face was red, blotchy, and still wet with tears when she eventually stood up and made her way behind the sofa. The base of the lamp had broken and shattered all over the floor. She just left it, and began to walk back to her bedroom. It was already dark outside and she just felt like calling it a day after breaking down. The sound of her cell phone's text message alert stopped her from walking down the hallway. She hadn't remembered leaving her phone on the kitchen table after she came inside, but that's where she found it.

There was a message from Quinn. *I'm sorry I was bitchy when you left. I just don't want to be here. Thanks for a fun few days.*

This was it. This was her pick-me-up, time to get-it-together-again, message. Quinn was oblivious, but this was her mother speaking through her. Quinn was Sax's reason. Sax needed to live for her. She was a blessing in her life. She needed her. They needed each other.

Sax smiled at her phone and that message from a twelve-year-old girl whom she'd loved since she met her as a baby-faced six year old, but loved even more now that she was all she had left of Jenner. Sax replied, *No worries, Quinnster. I can be bitchy too. I know you don't want to be there.* Sax wanted to add how she will do all she can, and more, to get her away from her father, but she didn't. She couldn't say that. She, would, however, do it. Then, she added, *Make the best of it for now. You don't have to thank me. I am here for you always. And I love you.*

Love you to, Quinn responded, and Sax was reminded by the misspelling that Quinn was still just a kid as she smiled at the phone in her hand.

* * *

Seth Moss was sitting behind his desk on the twenty-first floor of the Chicago high rise which housed the corporation that launched his career. It really was a dream job for Seth to punch keys and navigate the mouse in front of his computer each and every day. In some ways he felt like an investigator. There were idiots, as he called them, some brilliant, some not, hacking computer systems every single day. It was his job to keep people and companies safe and secure, or to help them regain that security. Seth's doctorate of philosophy in computer science landed him that job, but his hands-on experience over the course of nearly seven years was what formed him. He was the best that company had, and they were well aware of it. He was making more than two-hundred grand for his performance. And today he gained a new client.

Seth sat back in the large, black leather chair behind his desk after the phone rang and he put it to his ear. He listened first. He always listened before speaking. It was one of the qualities Sax had loved most about him. He didn't attempt to chime in or have all of the answers until he received all of the facts, or opinions. His steel blue, long-sleeved, button-down dress shirt was form fitting. It wasn't tight, but as he sat, the buttons pulled around his abs and broad chest. There wasn't an ounce of fat anywhere on that man's body. He listened to a young man explain how he didn't know a lot about computers. It wasn't his thing. Art was his craft. He was an oil painter, who earned a Masters of Fine Arts in figurative art from the New York Academy of Art. He only wanted to live out a dream and make a living doing what he loved. He found a website to download his paintings to display and sell, and someone had stolen all of them. There were only ten, and that was a lot to him as he had put his heart and soul into creating his best work. Someone else had thought the same. His work was worthy of recognition. It had caught someone's eye and was stolen. All of it was duplicated, mostly by merging paintings. The young man wanted help in tracking the man who already had made nine hundred thousand dollars at his expense. The thief wasn't too bright, or experienced, Seth was told on the phone, because he had placed and sold the newly crafted paintings as his own on a sister website to the one he had stolen the original paintings from. The young man told Seth his name was Jason Zimmer and he said he needed his help. To Seth, it was like seeking justice. He took his job seriously and quickly gained the trust of his clients because of that.

After several minutes of listening and punching the keys on the keyboard to form some notes on the computer screen in front of him, it was Seth's turn to ask questions. He rubbed his left hand over the top of his closely-shaved ash brown hair as he held the phone receiver in his right hand. "So, Mr. Zimmer, you do realize that because your paintings were not fully copyrighted, as you admitted, you cannot regain rights of them? They're gone. History. They may be in the hands of a thief who profited greatly, but they are no longer yours to claim. Are we clear on that?"

"Yes," the young artist replied, regretfully. "Unfortunately I've learned that in a very painful way. I'm calling you today for help in tracking down this coward who can't paint his own way to success. He used my paintings as a crutch. He's a criminal who will never be prosecuted, I know that. People like this get by with stealing all the time. I would just like a name to put to a face. Call it retaliation, I guess. An acquaintance told me about your firm and how it's your job to uncover the hackers."

"It is," Seth spoke again, "but your situation isn't really classified as such."

"No, but you're the closest thing I could find to do some computer undercover work, per se," Jason Zimmer said. He sounded young to Seth, but not as naïve as he originally gathered when he first began this phone conversation with him. This was simply a man, a talented man Seth assumed, pissed off that his work was stolen. Seth didn't know why, but he felt connected to this story and wanted to jump on this case. But, he knew his firm would not allow it. This was not what they did.

"I've turned away people like you numerous times, Mr. Zimmer," Seth began. "I'm not in a position to play catch-the-thief." Seth heard the young man sigh into the phone. "But, I would like to know where you are from?"

"Just outside of Chicago," Jason Zimmer replied as his curiosity peeked. "I live in Forest Park."

"I see," Seth smiled into the phone. "Then, it's your lucky day. What do you say you make that nineteen-minute commute to Gilt Bar on West Kinzie and meet me for a drink after work tonight?"

"I don't understand," Jason Zimmer started to say, but he stopped and rephrased his comment. "I mean, sure, yes, I'll be there."

"Five-thirty. I'm wearing a blue shirt, black dress pants, and I have a skinhead of brown hair." Seth was still smiling and feeling an unexplained excitement about helping out this kid, or so he sounded to be young over the phone reception. He wanted to go out of his way for him. Again, he didn't know why. He wouldn't be on company time, and he wasn't even concerned about making a profit off of this deal. That is, if he was able to help him. He certainly wanted to give it his best effort.

"I'll find you," Jason Zimmer said, sounding like a kid who feigned having confidence.

Seth walked into Gilt Bar with confidence. He'd been there before, numerous times to count, but that's how he made an entrance anywhere. He wasn't an arrogant man, but at first glance he could easily be judged as such. Once he spoke, however, any negative opinions quickly changed. He was kind and his ease with himself always quickly put others in a similar state. Seth Moss was easy to talk to. Easy to like. And, for some, easy to love. He had broken a few hearts in Chicago, too. He made a point to never get serious in a relationship again. Those words upfront, or after a sexual encounter, always resulted in a disappointed, brokenhearted woman who wanted to fall, or maybe had already fallen for him.

He sat down at the bar, after finding two vacant stools on one of the far ends. He caught the bartender's attention and ordered an Effen Black Cherry Vodka. It was the drink of choice for many Chicagoans. It's poured in a glass of Coke and basically the taste of Cherry Coke with alcohol.

After two sips, Seth slightly turned his bar stool to find a young man approaching him.

"Mr. Moss?" he asked.

"Zimmer?" Seth asked, offering his hand to a young man dressed in dark-washed jeans, a white long-sleeved button-down dress shirt and brown loafers on his feet. His jet black hair was brushed back on his head and it looked as if it was wet or had product in it.

"Yes, sir. It's a pleasure. Thank you for meeting me." Just as Seth had thought, Jason Zimmer was a young man. Early twenties, he guessed. He appeared to be of Taiwanese descent, but he spoke like an American. Maybe, a parental mix of both genes had resulted in this striking young man, Seth wondered. Not that it mattered, and Seth already liked him. He was green, but he was kind and obviously timid. He lacked confidence, Seth perceived, but he appeared to want to present himself as bigger than he felt. Maybe Seth was meant to be a mentor for this young man, he wondered. And he was flattered.

"Please, sit down. I'll order you a drink. What'll it be?" Seth asked him.

"Um, I'll have what you're having?" It sounded more like a question than a request and Seth contemplated just ordering the boy a Cherry Coke, straight up, and when the bartender responded to Seth's first attempt to gain his attention, he ordered the young artist a Cherry Coke.

Seth spoke again after a generous sip of his own drink. "I'll get right to the reason I asked you here. I want to help you. You have not hired me from the firm you made the phone call to today. As of right now, you have not hired me, solely, either." Jason Zimmer creased his brow. He didn't quite grasp what Seth was saying. "I don't want your money," Seth clarified, "but I do want to help you."

"For nothing?" the young man asked, now sounding more innocent than he wanted to.

"For gratification. To boost my own ego. To name and locate the coward, as you called him, who stole from you and reaped the benefits of your talent." Seth didn't just assume this artist before him had talent. He had already Googled him and saw firsthand that his paintings were striking. Not all of them were alike either as he painted a selection of human figures, portraits, still-life, and landscapes. Not that Seth was an expert on any type of artwork. He just simply liked what he saw. Raw talent was the best way he could describe the paintings that Jason Zimmer claimed were stolen. He may have earned the degree in college where he was expected to walk away trained and coached, but Seth believed a talent like his was natural born. His work looked as if he made up his own rules as he created.

"I don't know what to say," Jason Zimmer admitted. "I came in here nervous as hell, trying to put on a front. I'm not a cool guy, bursting at the seams with confidence like you are. I'm just a man who believes in my own talent." Seth was impressed with his honesty. His confession made him like this boy even more.

Chapter 7

Seth spent a few hours at Gilt Bar with Zimmer, as he now liked to call him. When the crowd dwindled, they found a corner table and Zimmer pulled out his laptop from his briefcase and presented Seth with a slideshow of the paintings which were stolen. Seth refrained from mentioning that he had already seen his paintings. What he had not seen was the stolen artist's version of the paintings. There were five of them, five merged scenes strategically painted with Zimmer's original detail. The copycat paintings were phenomenal, Seth thought, and it was obvious to him that the artist they would be looking for was experienced. This guy was very good. He had an eye for what needed to be brushed on canvas. He added more detail to Zimmer's paintings but what he stole from Zimmer was pertinent to make the five paintings complete. It was as if this artist, who was indeed a thief, needed a push, or inspiration, from someone else. Maybe he was burnt out on inspiration, Seth wondered, but kept his thought to himself.

"Let me see that, closer. Zoom in," Seth told Zimmer, to allow him to get a better look. "What is this?" Seth asked, pointing to the watermark on each of the five paintings.

"It's called a watermark," Zimmer explained. "It's a transparent marking that some artists apply to their work."

"As you should have done," Seth spoke to him like a father would to a son.

"Yeah, so I've learned," Zimmer sighed.

"Didn't learn shit in college, did you?" Seth asked him.

"Not really, I rarely showed up for class. Just painted at home in my studio and turned in the assignments. The professor didn't care. I earned the grades I needed to pass the classes."

"Well that's all wonderful, but just think how if you would have been present for a lecture or two, you may have picked up on how to protect your work, bozo." Seth smiled at Zimmer and they both chuckled. They liked each other.

"So, help me make this out," Seth said, trying not to admit in front of a young kid that he at thirty-one years old might need glasses. All the time spent in front of a computer screen was catching up to him.

"It's Z-Ski," Zimmer informed him.

"What?" Seth laughed out loud.

"And that's funny, why?" Zimmer asked him.

"Well, I'm assuming it's a pseudonym, but what's funny

is I grew up in Southern Illinois, Marion County to be exact. Marion bumps up against Clinton County, home of a citrus soda made from orange and lemon juices, and a thousand teaspoons of sugar. It's called Ski." Seth smiled and Zimmer raised his eyebrows.

"You're thinking there is a connection here, aren't you?" Zimmer asked him, already impressed with this man he wanted to know better.

"Not really, I don't know. The guy could live near the slopes too for all we know," Seth said, honestly. "If this is a fictitious name, as it most likely is, we could spin our wheels for months without answers. If this guy is like you and shouldn't be using J.Zimmer on his work until he's rich and famous," Seth shook his head at him, "we could find him pretty quickly. Like within the next ten minutes."

"I did Google Z.Ski, but the search was too broad all over the country," Zimmer told him.

"But, now, we may be able to start and end our search in Southern Illinois," Seth said, as Zimmer shook his head *yes* close to eight consecutive times. He was such a boy still.

All it took was logging onto whitepages.com and punching in Z.Ski under the name and the location as Illinois. The search did not come up empty. It revealed Zander Skissem in Peoria, Illinois, Zoe Skit in Elk Grove Village, Illinois, and Zane Ski in Salem, Illinois.

When Seth thought he saw Salem on the small laptop screen in a poorly lit bar, he asked Zimmer for sure. "What does that say? Salem, right?" Zimmer nodded his head again, remaining silent because he was afraid to hope that this search had been so effortless. All he really had to do was find the right man. Seth Moss was that man, and he had found him by pure, unbelievable luck. Or maybe it was fate?

"Salem is in Marion County, back to back with Clinton. This guy Ski was as stupid as you were. He used his real name on the paintings he's claiming as his own." Seth was certain they had found their man. The thief. He was somewhat taken aback that their search had been too easy, but he was more affected by the City of Salem resurrecting in his heart right now. He said he would never go back. There were too many memories there. Hurtful ones. He did wonder if she was still there. Sax Arynn probably had a new name by now. A married name. A few little ones were calling her mama too, he assumed. Damn, he was a fool. He had never tried to look her up. It would hurt too much to see she had moved on. Just sitting there thinking about her now was overwhelming him. He had ignored her calls, texts, and all attempts to reach out to him. To reconcile. Eventually, he changed his cell phone number.

"What's up with you?" Zimmer asked, recognizing how lost in thought he had so suddenly become.

"I was just thinking how living in Salem seems like a lifetime ago," Seth admitted.

"So you don't go home to visit much?" Zimmer inquired.

"No. Haven't been back since I left almost seven years ago. Nothing, no one left there to visit. My folks and I don't communicate much. They moved to Colorado five or six years ago. I haven't gone there either."

"That's a shame," Zimmer said. "I still live with my parents." Seth giggled. He wasn't surprised. "So when do we take our trip to your old hometown?" Zimmer quickly brought up the question. And he was serious. He wanted Seth to go with him. He wasn't sure what he would do once he was there and tracked down the artist who stole his paintings, but he just knew he had to go there and do this.

"Um, no. My job is done, pal," Seth spoke with certainty. "You are on your own. This search ended up being way too damn easy. I will take a little credit for narrowing you to Illinois, but my part goes no further."

"You can't do that!" Zimmer responded, feeling a little angry and probably more hurt than anything.

"I can and I will," Seth responded, feeling irked. No one was going to make him go back. He lived a new life now. There was no going back. *Why would he want to purposely trek that path back to her? Did he have to see for himself how she was able to move on and be happy without him?* It's what he had told her to do when he left. It was ironically what he thought he would be able to do.

"I'll pay you to go along with me, I'll pay your travel expenses, too," Zimmer offered.

"I told you I don't want or need your money," Seth was adamant.

"Then just do it for me," Zimmer said, with an honesty Seth again admired about him.

"What?" Seth asked him.

"Come on, you can't sit here and tell me you don't feel it, too?" Zimmer asked.

"Feel what?" Seth asked, thinking maybe he should feign being uncomfortable and just leave.

"This connection, this bond, this vibe. I think you're incredibly awesome. I'd like to get to know you better, you know, be friends."

Seth laughed. He did like this kid. "I think you're pretty fucking awesome yourself."

"So that means this isn't the end of our journey?" Zimmer asked, sounding a little too philosophical for Seth's liking.

"What are you gay?" Seth asked, in a completely joking manner. He had both gay and lesbian friends. They were wonderful people. He had nothing against them. He was just simply making a joke, and then he realized it wasn't a joke.

"As a matter of fact, yes, I am," Zimmer replied, and for the first time all night, Seth noticed a sincere confidence in this young man. He may have believed in himself as an artist, but it was obvious he was entirely content, and proud, to admit he was gay.

"Holy shit, really?" Seth giggled. "Are you interested in me? Because, back off bud, I'm into women and only women."

This time it was Zimmer's turn to giggle. "Can I slide over on the chair closest to you?" he teased. "I really would like to put my hands on you...and those tight pecks."

"Ugh, you fucker!" Seth smiled, and Zimmer smiled right back at him. They were instant friends and Zimmer knew it would only be a matter of time before he convinced Seth Moss to return to Salem, Illinois with him.

✳ ✳ ✳

Sax pulled up alongside the road in front of the old mansion. This time she was showing up unexpected. It was Friday night, she was on her way home from work and she wanted to stop in to see Quinn, with hope that she would be able to snatch her away for the night. A girl's night appealed to her. She sat in her car for a few minutes, with both of the front windows rolled all the way down. The air was brisk, but it felt good to her. She dragged on the last of her cigarette and threw it out the driver's side window before she stepped out of the car and slammed the door. The wrap-around porch with those four white large round pillars was lit up so she assumed they were home.

When she reached the front door in her skinny black pants, charcoal gray boots with a two-inch pointy heel, and a thick, warm, white turtleneck sweater, Sax rang the bell. She waited, but no one came. She was bold then and opened the door. As she peeked only her head inside first, she heard Zane yell, "I'm in the studio, be right up!" She knew Zane's art studio was downstairs and she also knew how he loathed when anyone saw his artwork in progress. This time, she respected that as she stepped into the living room, shut the front door behind her, and waited there. A moment later, she heard him climbing the stairs. Probably taking two steps at a time in those black Army boots of his, she thought, feeling like rolling her eyes.

When the basement door near the stairway opened, he saw Sax and his face all but dropped. It was obvious to her that he was expecting someone else. "Sax? I didn't–"

"I know, I've shown up unannounced," she said to him, without apologizing. "Is Quinn here?"

"No, she's at a sleepover tonight," he informed her and Sax felt left out. She wanted to know when Quinn had plans. She hadn't made too many plans in recent months since Jenner died. A part of Sax was happy to hear Quinn was getting back into living how she used to, but another side of her wasn't thrilled. She wanted Quinn's free time to be spent with her. It was as if she was feeling like a mother of a preteen who knew all too well that her little girl was growing up and enjoying time away from her. "I thought you were the UPS man. I'm expecting a delivery and it's late."

"No brown man here," Sax teased, making a joke about the delivery uniforms that the United Parcel Service employees have worn for decades.

Zane smiled and actually chuckled a bit under his breath. That's when she noticed he was holding a longneck bottle of beer. He always looked the same, in his black jeans, paint-spattered white t-shirt, tattooed arms of course, and so nothing different or out of the ordinary ever caught her eye. But, the beer did now. And he noticed her staring. "Can I get you a drink?" he asked, and for some reason Sax liked the polite side of him. It was a welcomed change.

"Um, no, like I said, I just stopped by for Quinn..." she stuttered the words and nervously brushed away the hair over her right eye with a swipe of her hand.

"Doesn't mean you can't stay for a drink," Zane pressed.

"Right, but–" Sax began to say, and Zane took a few steps toward the kitchen.

"Be right back with your beer," he said, and then he was gone.

Sax enjoyed beer, and accepted the cold bottle from him when he returned. "Thank you," she said, as he handed it to her and then walked over and plopped down on the burnt orange leather sofa. That's when Sax noticed he had new furniture. That color was not one she would have chosen. He sure had ugly taste in furniture, she thought to herself, as he invited her to take a seat. All he had in that room to sit down on was the burnt orange leather sofa, and there was an oval-shaped glass-topped coffee table in front of it. She wished he had ordered a matching chair now, in any freaking color, because sitting next to him on the sofa didn't appeal to her. *Maybe drinking that beer would help.*

An hour passed and the conversation was surprisingly easy as they spoke about Quinn, Sax's career at the hospital, and his art. The beers were going down quite easily too, as Zane just returned from the kitchen with Sax's third and his fifth. He had been drinking in his studio prior to Sax's unexpected visit.

"This is my last one," she said, trying to sound serious. "I have to drive home...soon." They both thought of the same thing when she spoke those words. She was tipsy and he was drunk but they shared a look of sadness and regret, knowing drinking and then driving drunk was what had taken Jenner away from them. Zane may never have had Jenner in his life, but she was linked to him because they were Quinn's parents. Sax was thinking how Jenner never wanted him to be a father to their daughter, and she spoke those words.

"Did you hate her?" Sax asked.

"No," Zane replied, knowing exactly who she was referring to. "I could never have hated her." He grew silent and Sax stood up from the sofa and walked over to the painting she purposely had not glanced at all evening. Zane watched her move across the room and because he was intoxicated, he didn't have anything sarcastic or mean to say to her about staying away from the painting. The last time he caught her in front of it, staring, and thinking, he panicked. He didn't want her to know. Now, he knew she already did.

Sax kept her back to Zane as she stood directly in front of that painting. *Damn, he really did a flawless job of painting Jenner.* That was her, in vivid detail. Sax stared longer and wondered if she stared long enough would she have the power in her eyes, and in her heart, to bring Jenner to life? Back to life. If only she could just move within that painting. *Smile. Talk to me. I miss you like pure hell, my friend.*

Zane never said a word, he just kept tipping back his fifth bottle of beer until he emptied it. Sax, after what felt like endless minutes, turned around finally. "Why did you paint this?" she asked, solemnly.

"What do you mean?" Zane asked, slurring his words. "I paint whatever the fuck I want to paint. What I know. What I see. What I feel…in my heart." He beat his hand loudly against his chest.

"What did you feel for her?" Sax asked, calmly and sincerely. "I see Jenner in this painting. It's amazing and so real. And that man, is not you, he doesn't look at all like you, but really it is, isn't' it?" Sax was tipsy enough to ask him anything. And she just had.

"I've never in my life painted anything with more soul," Zane admitted, leaning forward on the sofa and resting his elbows on his knees. "She didn't want me. She never did. We shared this wild chemistry that one night at a hotel downtown St. Louis, not too far from the museum where we met. I could have made love to her over and over again all night long. She was done with me after one time. And that was our story. She was done with me." Sax was listening intently. Jenner used to speak of him as just that. She knew as soon as she had sex with him that it had been a mistake. She never once called her daughter a mistake though. She felt confident about being a single mother and she wanted Zane Ski to have no part of his daughter's life. But, he wouldn't leave her alone. She had made the mistake of telling him what city she lived in during their conversation at the art museum and before their foreplay started in a corridor of that museum. Days afterward, he tracked her down. He called her repeatedly at work because she never shared her cell phone number with him, and finally she had threatened to have the police issue a restraining order against him. He backed off, but continued to follow her. He didn't contact her, he only watched her. After four months, he could plainly see that she was pregnant. That's when he made his presence known again. And that's when Jenner, in turn, took legal measures and a restraining order was issued against him. He went back to his apartment in St. Louis then, and never contacted her again. He kept tabs on her through the years, and even asked a favor of his private investigator friend who supplied him with pictures of his daughter every year on her birthday. And then, twelve years later, he made the move to Salem to be a father to his daughter when her mother died. Jenner had messed up. She thought Zane was out of her life and would never be in their daughter's life. She thought she was in control, but there was no plan in place if she were to die. Quinn met her father the day after her mother's funeral. She didn't love him. She didn't even like him. But, he loved her, just as much as he had her mother.

"We all have our own pain," Sax said to him, again with sincerity in her voice. "I am so caught up in this painting," she said, turning around to face it again.

"Thank you," he said, wishing he had another beer to slam down so he could forget what he just admitted to her. He had never told anyone. Jenner thought he was a loser, and that broke him to his very core.

"I mean it," Sax said, referring to the painting again. "I want this, or a duplicate of it." As she spoke, she reached both of her arms up and attempted to take down the frame from hanging on the wall. Zane immediately stood up. But, he was too late. Sax had already moved and discovered that the painting wasn't just a frame hanging on a nail or by a fancy hardwire stretched across the back of the frame. It was a door. The left side of the frame was on hinges and it opened just a like a door to reveal a large combination knob behind it. Sax was staring in confusion now at what looked like a safe. It was being hidden behind the painting.

"What is this?" she asked, as Zane was immediately too close behind her. He reached his long, tattooed arm over her as he stood at six-foot-two and she at five-seven. He didn't slam it shut, but came close as the frame again was sealed against the wall. It was obviously protecting, hiding, something Zane did not want her to see.

"None of your business," he said, as he looked down at her and she was looking at him. She could feel his breath on her face and smelled beer. The beer they both had been drinking. The effects of that alcohol consumption lead to Zane coming downward and Sax moving upward, and their lips met with force. It wasn't passion, but there was desire evident that nearly threw them both for a loop. *Had they even liked each other?* He kissed her hard, open-mouthed, full tongue, and she responded aggressively. She could smell the shampoo in his long hair that used to repulse her just to look at. And he was wearing cologne near his face and neck that smelled good enough to taste. Her hands were wrapped around the base of his neck and moving upward through his hair. While kissing her, he started to move his hands as well. Before she knew it, she was allowing him to touch her breasts underneath her fluffy white turtleneck sweater. He pulled it up high enough to see her now. She looked at him with drunk eyes, but there was approval in them. He quickly lifted her sweater up and over her head. She peeled off his t-shirt and nearly ripped it. It was a thin piece of material and when it came off, she saw another tattoo across his left breast. It was the woman in the painting. It was Jenner. A complete replica of Jenner from the woman depicted on the frame on the wall near them. Sax stared at it for a moment. God, she missed her. And as strange as it was, she wanted to be close to Jenner again by getting as close as she could to this man right now. They shared a love for that woman, and Sax wanted to forget her pain this instant. She wanted to feel with her body and her soul exactly what Zane felt. They both had loved Jenner.

Zane pulled her down roughly to the floor beneath the painting. Her bra came off. He touched her breasts, he kissed them with a force that seemed animal-like. He was devouring her, and Sax was so turned on and responding to his every wild, rough move. Her boots were thrown across the room, one by one, and her tight pants were pulled off inside-out by the time they reached her ankles. His boots met hers on the floor. His belt and jeans were scattered elsewhere. He was wearing no underwear and hers were in his hands as he moved his mouth between her legs. He moved up to her face to kiss her again, full on the mouth and she reached down for his manhood. He was a man with a skinny, but incredibly strong body. And when he entered her and rocked over her repeatedly with his knees planted on the hardwood floor, Sax felt pleasured over and over. He was rough and she took it and climaxed with him inside of her. He had stamina like she never experienced before. By the time he came inside of her, he moaned loudly as she watched the sweat drip off his long locks. Somehow his long ponytail had come out during sex and his hair was all over the place. Long and wild, and so unlike Sax's short-cropped style.

When he pulled himself out of her, she felt like she had just gone through an out-of-body experience and suddenly had snapped harshly back to reality. *What the hell had she just done? What the hell had they just done together?* She took both of her hands, opened her palms, and pushed him off of her by his chest. He fell over her body and beside her on the floor.

She rushed to gather her clothes, putting most of it on as quickly as she possibly could. It wasn't easy with skinny pants and she ended up wearing her sweater backwards without a bra, no panties, and carrying her boots as she ran out of the front door. The last thing, and only thing, she heard him yell after her was, *You wanted it too!*

Chapter 8

Sax stood in the shower for over an hour. The steaming hot water was pouring over her body and her skin had reddened. She wanted to wash and rinse it all off. His hands. His mouth. His body. All of him and what had taken place between them. She was sick to her stomach over what she had allowed to happen.

By the time she finally turned off the shower water, Sax wrapped her hair in a fluffy white towel and slipped on her white fleece robe and tied it tightly around her waist. She walked into her bedroom and sat down on the bed, against the headboard and on her pillow. She pulled her knees up to her chest, and cried. This was what grief had done to her. She couldn't think straight. The alcohol hadn't helped to keep her focused and sane either. But, it was that painting that set her off, spinning out of control. She was out of her mind when she believed she wanted to be with Zane in the closest, most physical way, just to feel close to Jenner again. It was sickening to her. Repulsive. And she was beating herself up about it right now. It was done. Over. And there was nothing she could do to reverse what happened. And she wanted so much to be able to talk to Jenner. So she did.

"Hey…how badly have I screwed up? Pardon the pun," she added, not wanting to smile but she did. "I don't know what I was thinking. Well, I do know, and I'm so weirded out right now. Just be with me. Forgive me. Help me to forgive myself…and forget that it happened. I need you in my life. I'm so lost without your guidance. Dammit, Jenner! I love you and miss you so fucking much. I just wanted to stop the hurt!" Sax started crying again and when she finally took a deep breath, she was startled to find a heavy scent in the air surrounding her on the bed. There was no mistake. It was Jenner's perfume. She, and it was so ironic now, had only worn Angel by Thierry Mugler.

"Oh my God…" she said aloud, looking around, hoping to see Jenner. She wanted to see her, halo and all. "Are you here?" There was silence, and Sax never saw anything in her bedroom, but she continued to breathe the scent of Angel in the air and she felt at peace as she knew for certain she felt Jenner's presence.

Sax kept breathing in as much of the scent as she could. She disturbed her natural breathing process, not exhaling enough air before inhaling again. She kept talking to Jenner, too. And by midnight, she had worn herself out and fallen asleep on top of her bedding in her robe with the towel still wrapped around her wet head. She would remember it all in the morning, including the peaceful feeling Jenner had brought to her from the other side. What was done was over, and it was time to move on. Again.

✳ ✳ ✳

Two days later, Sax had to face him again. Quinn was going to spend a couple days and nights with her, so she had to go back to that old mansion to pick her up. She had to face walking inside that front door, which she bolted out of last time in a state of full regret.

Her heels were planted on that old front porch, which creaked in places beneath her. Sax took a deep breath before she rang the bell. Quinn was never ready on time, so she knew she couldn't expect to meet her at the door and turn around and get the hell out of there. *What was she allowing to happen here? She was Sax Arynn, a woman who had been to hell and back. Suck it up and move on.* She looked down at her feet and her hair hung further over her right eye. And then she lifted up her chin, slowly inhaled the cold outside air through her nostrils, and forced herself to press her finger to that rusty doorbell.

"Come in!" she heard Quinn's voice through the door. Sax turned the knob, opened the door, and stepped inside. She looked up to find Quinn leaning over the balcony upstairs. Her long blonde hair was down and hanging forward as she bent over the railing. "Be ready soon, okay?" Quinn told Sax, but didn't wait for her reply as she ran off, down the hallway upstairs, and into her bedroom. Sax assumed she wasn't finished packing.

She purposely didn't move from standing right in front of the door. *Maybe Zane wasn't home? Or maybe he was in full artist mode in the basement studio?* Sooner or later, Sax knew she would have to see him. But, now, purposely trying not to glance over at the hardwood floor beneath that painting, she hoped for later.

Luck, however, never seemed to be on her side. Sax could hear Quinn walking around upstairs as she was getting ready, but in closer proximity she heard footsteps climbing the basement stairs. She watched the closed door leading down to the basement swing open and he saw her at the same time she saw him. And that's when the confident and secure image which Sax Arynn always strived to possess, surfaced.

"Sax, hi, I've been expecting you. I mean, for Quinn." Zane seemed nervous, but making an effort to be kind, which was unusual for him.

"Yep, I'm here and on time, unlike Quinnster." It was always easier to joke when she was nervous.

"She must get that from her mother," Zane stated, and Sax thought, *why bring up Jenner?* The last time that led the two of them to serious trouble. And regret. Sax only smiled a little.

"I think I'm going to go upstairs to see what's keeping Quinn," Sax spoke as she began walking toward the staircase and away from where she had not moved an inch from standing by the door. But, first, she had to get past Zane.

He never moved aside when she reached him. "About what happened–"

"No," Sax interrupted him. "Nothing happened. There's no need to discuss, rehash, or go there ever again. We were drunk." And that was all Sax said to him as she pushed past him, knocking her shoulder into his arm in order to get by and onto the bottom step leading upstairs.

✳ ✳ ✳

"So how are you really doing?" Sax asked Quinn after they had eaten cheeseburgers and French Fries and each drank a Coke at a local restaurant and drove home. Quinn was lounging on the pale yellow sofa and Sax sat down beside her feet.

"I'm okay," she replied, not really wanting Sax to go there. They had fun together, and she liked when Sax talked about her mother and shared things she had said or they had done together. But, Quinn didn't want to talk about how much she missed her or how bad the pain felt, day in and day out. She truly wondered if she would feel this way the rest of her life. *Would missing her mother ever get easier?*

"I know we don't talk about this," Sax began, carefully, "but since you refused counseling at school and professionally, I feel like it's always going to be my job to be here for you if you want to talk. It may not be right now, or even this year. You may be married with a baby on the way someday and realize you want to, or need to, find a way to heal your soul before you become a mother yourself."

Quinn smiled at that thought. "That's a long time from now," she said to Sax.

"Yes, I hope so," Sax grinned, "but in any case, I'm just trying to make a point. We all need to face pain, eventually." It truly was ironic for Sax to be preaching those words when she was far from living by them. She never faced the pain of losing Seth, and now again with Jenner her bottled up emotions were reaching the boiling point but she wasn't giving in. Both Sax and Quinn would benefit from seeking the help of a therapist.

"Sax, can I say something without making you mad?" Quinn asked.

"Of course," Sax responded, grabbing Quinn's feet through the black and orange Nike Elite socks she was wearing. "You know me better than that."

"My mom always said you were strong, invincible, and courageous. She loved those qualities about you," Quinn stated, and Sax showed no emotion, but she wanted to hear more. *What else did your mom used to say about me?* "But, she also said so much of that was a cover. She said your heart had been through too much ache and if you didn't allow yourself to feel and then heal, you would end up sad and alone for the rest of your life."

Sax giggled a little. "I loved your mom, but I hated how wise she was." Both of them laughed together. "Seriously, Quinn, she was right, and I learned so much from her in the six years we were the best of friends. She helped me through some rough patches and now I want to be here to do the same for you."

"You're a great friend…and mom," Quinn said, and then she added, just for complete clarification, "to me." This time Sax didn't feel, or act, so tough. Tears sprung to her eyes and she got up and sat back down closer to Quinn's chest. Quinn sat up to meet her for that hug they both needed.

When they separated, they were both teary. "I don't want to talk about how empty this feels," Quinn told Sax as she remained sitting close to her while she laid back down on her back. A few tears spilled from the outer corners of her eyes and trickled down her cheeks. "I don't want to talk about how scary it is being twelve years old and still feeling like a kid, but knowing I have to grow up because I no longer have my mom to take care of everything, and of me." Sax allowed Quinn to keep talking. Each time she said, *I don't want to talk,* she ultimately revealed more of how she was really feeling. "I think it sucks. I am mad at her for drinking and driving. She was supposed to be an adult. She set rules for me to follow, why couldn't she obey that one very important rule that could have saved her life? I am mad at God for allowing this to happen. Why did he have to take *my* mom when she was all I had?"

Sax gave Quinn some time to continue, and when she didn't, she spoke to her. "All of what you just shared with me is a lot to process. You *are* just a kid and you should not have to deal with any of that. But, honey, unfortunately this is life. Life is damn hard and so unfair at times, but we have no choice but to roll with it. I know how empty you feel. I know you're scared. I am, too. But, I can help you, we can help each other. Hold tight to me and this gradually may not seem as scary for both of us. I was drinking too that night. It was stupid of both of us, but we had done it so many times and nothing had happened." Sax refrained from mentioning that she had just driven tipsy again a few nights ago after she left Zane at the old mansion. That thought still made her sick to her stomach. "We all make choices and at the time we are choosing, I believe, we are doing what we want to do. It's afterward, when things go terribly wrong or when we are unhappy, that we start to regret and we accuse ourselves or each other of making the wrong choice."

"I think you're all the therapy I'm gonna need," Quinn said, wiping the tears off of her face simultaneously with both of her hands.

Sax smiled at Quinn and took both of her damp hands in her own. "I will always listen. I will always try to help you with how you're feeling by sharing how I perceive things or how I attempt to handle my own crazy emotions. I am not perfect, but I love you and I loved your mother so much. We were soul sisters. Not being here for you is something I cannot fathom. You, my dear, are my life."

"Mom used to say that you needed to get a life," Quinn teased her.

"Oh I know," Sax giggled. "I used to dish that shit right back to her. But, you know, all we both really cared about was each other… and you."

Chapter 9

It was only one week since Seth had uncovered the name of the man who had stolen and sold Zimmer's paintings as his own. And, now, as Seth sat behind his desk looking out the window of the Chicago high rise, he received a third text in three days asking him to agree to a trip to Salem. Seth shook his head when he saw that it was Zimmer again, and he put his phone back down on the desk and resumed watching the snow come down. The flakes were large and coming down so heavy that the entire city was difficult to make out as anything more than just white. At least three or four inches were on the ground already, and that much more was expected from this snowstorm. Seth's cell phone ringing now broke his concentration.

He answered on the second ring. "Zimmer! How the heck are you?" he asked him.

"I'd be better if you'd answer my texts," Zimmer began. "Join me for the trip. Come on, I'll pay for your plane ticket."

"No one is flying anywhere," Seth stated. "It's only a four-hour drive from here."

"Oh," Zimmer responded. "Does that mean you're agreeing to take a road trip with me?"

Seth smiled into the phone, but then he grew serious and asked Zimmer what he really planned to do once he got to Salem and located Zane Ski.

"What do you mean?" Zimmer asked, sounding nervous. "I want to confront him."

Again, Seth smiled. Zimmer was so naïve. "And you plan to say what? You can accuse him of stealing your paintings and he will deny it. Why drive all the way there for nothing? I don't understand your reasoning behind this," Seth admitted. "Just Google his image, print out his picture and throw darts at it or whatever suits you."

Seth was joking, but Zimmer didn't find it funny. He had already done that computer search and printed Zane Ski's photograph. Burning it afterward was what suited him. "Are you still there?" Seth asked him on the phone. "I was joking…"

"Yeah, I'm here, and I know you were," Zimmer told him. "Just do this with me, please. Man to man, artist to artist, I want to talk to Zane Ski. I have a feeling he'll never steal my paintings again if I'm given that chance."

Seth wanted to laugh out loud, but he didn't. He could just imagine Zimmer at five-foot, seven inches tall with very little muscle on his one-hundred-fifty-pound frame, trying to stand up to a man who was probably taller and stronger. But, Seth didn't mock his new friend. He just told him again that he would not be going back to Salem. *Not in this lifetime*, he thought to himself.

"I don't think we met just because I found your business number in the yellow pages," Zimmer said to Seth. "I think you're supposed to go back there. Maybe we are both looking for some sort of closure in that city?" Seth stared out the window that spanned the entire wall of his office. The wind had picked up and the snow was coming down sideways and blowing directing toward and onto the window he was now standing in front of. There was only glass separating him from the storm outside. He always preferred to stay on the safe side, error on the side of caution. Stay away from the edge. Run before you get in too deep. Commitment, in particular, scared the hell out of him. He knew that's why he left Sax, choosing to chase a career dream because it was just easier than committing to her and their relationship. He watched his parents stay committed in a loveless marriage all of his life. They tried counseling, retreats, and for better or worse neither one of them would ever give up. Some would admire their dedication, their will to hang in there. Seth thought they were both crazy. They were not happy together. Miserable was more like it.

"What makes you think I need closure?" Seth asked, seriously wondering if maybe Zimmer was right. "Maybe he needed to see for himself that Sax was happy and fulfilled in her life. Maybe then he could begin to be, too. He didn't know how to move on. He knew that now.

"You tell me," Zimmer replied. "Do you?" Zimmer held his breath. He felt as if he was onto something here. He saw it that night in Gilt Bar when the City of Salem appeared on the laptop screen. There was something in Seth's eyes. A reason he had not gone back to Salem since he moved to Chicago almost seven years ago.

"You're a pesty son of a bitch, you know that," Seth said, stretching his lower back as stood with the phone still up to his ear. His fitted long-sleeved white dress shirt was wrinkled in the back from sitting at his desk most of the day. "I'll drive," he added.

"What? Oh man! This is so awesome! You're awesome! Thank you so much, Seth. I mean that, thank you!" Zimmer again sounded like a kid and Seth only shook his head, thinking how he hoped with all of his being that he would not regret this decision. He was going back home.

✳✳✳

Sax was having difficulty finding the vein in the arm of a patient who had come to the lab for blood withdrawal. Her arms were thin and felt frail, and Sax knew she had been to the lab frequently in recent months. She was younger than Sax, probably mid twenties, and she was sickly. Sax thought Rue had mentioned some type of cancer, but she didn't recall for sure. Rue was always gossiping and that never failed to unnerve Sax. She hated small town gossip. Let people just live their lives. She personally struggled with the whispers when Seth dumped her and left town. Eventually, another story came along and someone else was the subject. "I'm sorry, honey, I'll try your other arm and if I can't find the vein, I'm going to get another tech in here who will hopefully have instant luck." Sax watched the young woman nod her head as her eyes teared up. Sax tapped two fingers on the woman's opposite arm, sterilized that specific spot with a cotton ball soaked with rubbing alcohol and then she instantly pushed her needle through the skin and into the visible vein. *Thank God.*

When the woman left, Sax just stood there. Life was so unfair. So many struggles. So much uncertainty. Sax forced herself to think about Quinn and how she was blessed to have her. They were blessed to have each other. She was the good in her life.

"What has you so lost in thought?" Rue asked, pulling the curtain back entirely as she entered the tiny room.

"Nothing," Sax responded, looking at her supervisor stuffed in her white lab coat. Her gray hair looked whiter to Sax for some reason right now. It was too short, too, as Sax noticed a fresh haircut that made her eyebrows stand out more than usual. Sax had short hair, but she preferred to keep it full on the top and hanging down to meet, and sometimes cover, her right eye.

"It's sad to see her come in here, isn't it?" Rue was jumping on the gossip wagon again.

"You never know what others are going through," Sax responded.

"They say her prognosis isn't good…" Rue started to talk.

"Who the hell is *they* anyway?" Sax snapped. "She's young, she will fight her disease."

"It's cancer," Rue pressed.

"Yeah," Sax responded with a tone that would have alerted anyone else to the brush off, but not Rue.

"There was a man in here asking about you yesterday afternoon after you left," Rue told Sax, changing the subject which had obviously upset her. Rue wondered if maybe Sax had lost someone to cancer in her lifetime. Once affected, personally or with loved ones, it changed people.

"A man?" Sax asked, uninterested.

"Yes, I told him you were gone for the day," Rue stated, "and he seemed disappointed. "Are you seeing anyone?"

"Seeing? As in dating? Rue, seriously, would I tell you if I was?" Sax smirked as she spoke. She didn't want to be unkind, but this woman unnerved her daily.

Rue laughed out loud. "Well, I'll take that as a *no*, and I admit I'm a bit relieved. That man looked skuzzy!" Sax had a baffled look on her face, and she never asked her to explain her comment, but Rue did anyway. "Tattoos on both arms, you could hardly see any skin! Oh, and that long hair in a ponytail. Grossed me out, for sure. Someone from the lab said he's an artist, the father of Jenner's child, maybe?"

Sax was upset now. "Rue! Really? If you knew who was here, why didn't you just come right out and say it? His name is Zane Ski. I have no idea why he would be looking for me here at the hospital. We deal with each other only when it concerns

Quinn." Sax wondered why she was telling her all of this. Probably because she really didn't want her to think she was involved with a man like Zane. *Sex one time hardly meant involved.*

"He just creeped me out a bit and I wanted you to know he was here, that's all," Rue said, feigning an innocence that Sax could see right through. But, she let her get by with it.

"I understand. Thanks," was all Sax said before she stepped out of the room, saying she was going to take a smoke break.

Chapter 10

It wasn't what Seth wanted to do, but he did feel somewhat compelled to just do it. He was driving on Interstate 57 in his black Ford Explorer, packed with only enough to get him through the weekend. Zimmer was sitting in the passenger seat and had not stopped talking since they left Chicago. Seth enjoyed his company, but his thoughts throughout this drive were focused on his decision to return to a city he lived in and, at one time, believed he'd never leave.

It was going on seven o'clock in the evening and they had driven nonstop from Chicago, where they left right from Seth's office at three in the afternoon. Their plan was to drive to the Salem Inn and Suites, just off of Route 50, where Seth had made reservations. It would be odd for him to stay in a hotel in Salem, but this whole trip was going to feel strange. Unlike Zimmer, who wanted to *look up* Zane Ski and who knew what he would say to him, if he confronted him, Seth had mixed emotions about looking up Sax. He believed she wouldn't want to see him. *Maybe he would just drive by her house?* He debated on searching for her to locate a current address. He assumed her name had changed, so Arynn would be all he had to go on. He could have looked her up on Facebook, but he hadn't done that in years. He didn't want to see her profile picture with someone new. A part of him hoped they would be back on the road to Chicago sooner than Sunday afternoon.

Seth was thinking of all the times Sax had texted him following his move to Chicago. He ignored every single one. There were many, at least weekly for a couple of months, and then they were sporadic before finally ceasing altogether. Most were just one line or two, he remembered clearly. *Happy Birthday. Hope all is well.* There were never pleas for him to come back to her, only thinking-of-you phrases. Seth knew if he had responded he would have given her hope, so he never did.

"You're quiet," Zimmer said to him as they reached the Salem city limits.

"Lots of memories here," Seth responded.

"What was her name?" Zimmer finally asked him.

Seth smiled. Men knew. Even a gay man knew that some women were just unforgettable. "Sax Arynn."

"Oh, she sounds feisty, sassy, sexy," Zimmer snapped his fingers back and forth in front of his own face after the mention of each adjective.

"All of the above," Seth responded, "and beautiful, too."

"I guess I don't have to ask," Zimmer stated. "She broke your heart, didn't she?"

"I wish that were true," he answered, thinking how that would at least be easier to take all these years later. Seth glanced at his surroundings in a town that hadn't changed all that much in several years and, he added, "I stomped all over hers."

"You sound like an asshole," Zimmer said, seriously.

"I'm sure she thinks that of me," Seth confessed. "But, thanks. I'm filled with enough regret."

"Regret, schmet!" Zimmer stated. "It's a waste of time and good energy. Make a change if you can. If not, let it be."

Seth was silent as they made their way to the Salem Inn. It was too late to make a change. He was certain of that. Too much time, too many years had passed. *Let it be?* He tried.

✳ ✳ ✳

Sax was at work by seven o'clock the next morning. She sometimes worked odd hours, or long hours, and today she would clock a twelve-hour shift in the lab performing microscopic, bacteriological, and chemical tests. Her job didn't end with blood withdrawal. Sax specialized in lab testing which led her to analysis of the tests to provide relevant results pertaining to diagnosis, prevention, and treatment of diseases.

She was perched up on a stool, pushed up against a long, rectangular shaped glass table in that sterile environment. Her white lab coat was unbuttoned and hung open, draping over the sides of the stool she sat on. She had gloves on her hands as she worked, deciphering the blood group and blood type to aide in a successful blood transfusion for a patient suffering from a severe disease. Not a day went by when she didn't think about how fortunate she was to have her health. So many people did not see the importance of living for each day. They were looking forward to Friday, or to summer, or to falling in love so they could be complete and happy. Sax didn't do that. She wasn't looking for anything more. Jenner had taught her how to appreciate each day for what it was. Life was so hard now for Sax without Jenner and her optimism, but she was trying.

Her cell phone buzzed in the front pocket of her lab coat, and Sax stepped away from the lab table and removed her gloves. She disposed of them in a sterile bin before she reached for her cell phone. *We need to talk.* Those were the only words in Zane's message. Sax hesitated to reply, but she did because she considered Quinn. That message could concern her. She texted back, *Is this about Quinn?* and pressed send. His response was only, *Yes.* So Sax, once again, replied to him, *At work. Will stop by tonight.*

***

85

"All I wanna do for now is drive by," Zimmer said to Seth as they had just eaten a continental breakfast at the hotel and walked outside to Seth's vehicle.

"I still can't believe his address is that old museum which was built in 1852," Seth stated. "That place was vacant for decades. I'll actually be curious to see if it still looks rundown from the outside. Maybe this guy put some real money into it?" Zimmer didn't say anything, but he was thinking any money Zane Ski recently pocketed was because he had stolen his creations. Zimmer didn't care if Ski had merged the paintings to get a different end result. The original idea was still his.

They drove three and a half miles through historic Salem, and ended up on the east edge of town. Seth drove by the old mansion slowly. They saw a tarnished white Mustang parked alongside of the road, but there was no activity. "Do you think he's home?" Zimmer asked. "Like, maybe, that's his car there?"

"I still don't know what you want to say to the guy?" Seth said, slowly passing the house and driving toward a dead end where he was going to turn around and creep by the house again for Zimmer. "Are you seriously going to just go up there, ring the bell, and accuse the man of stealing art?"

"I know what I need to do," Zimmer replied, staring blankly and straight ahead, and Seth felt uncomfortable.

"Well, here's the place. It's three and a half miles from our hotel. I'm not waiting while you punch the shit out of this guy. You're on your own if you come back later." Seth was partly teasing, but he had begun to feel uneasy about Zimmer's intentions. He was just a scrawny kid trying to jumpstart his dream of becoming somebody in the world of art. Seth enjoyed his company. Zimmer was clever and witty, and fun to be around. But, there was something distant in his eyes since they arrived in Salem. Seth liked this kid better when he wasn't so focused on art and what had happened to his first collection of masterpieces, as he repeatedly called them.

"You're right. Let's just drive," Zimmer said, forcing himself out of the trance he seemed to be in. "What about checking out some of those museums in St. Louis?" It was a ninety-minute drive from Salem to St. Louis, but Seth didn't mind. There were no friends he wanted to look up in Salem, and he was trying not to think about locating Sax. He, like Zimmer, might just want to find out where she lives and do a drive-by.

"I will take you to one, or maybe two, museums in St. Louis. You can see The Arch, too, if you want," Seth told him, "but, what I want, is to eat on The Hill. It's been a long time."

"What's The Hill?" Zimmer asked.

"A neighborhood within St. Louis that's located on high ground south of Forest Park, not the city you live in," Seth clarified with a smile. "The Hill has an Italian American majority population, and it's noted for Italian restaurants. We are so eating that food today. For me, that'll be worth a boring day spent at museums." Zimmer laughed out loud as Seth drove them out of Salem.

Chapter 11

It was already dark and the night air was cold as Sax parked her car, curbside, and walked up to Zane's house. This time, she didn't get up to the door to ring the bell before Zane opened it.

"Oh, hi, anxious?" she asked him as he stood there in black jeans, back boots, and a clean white t-shirt. His hair was again pulled back into a low ponytail. His face looked clean-shaven today and Sax couldn't remember if it always did. Not that it mattered. *He* didn't matter to her.

"Well, yeah, you said after work and that's been hours," Zane said, stepping back for her to enter the house. She was hoping for warmth in there, because it was cold outside, but that building was old and the ceilings were so high that it was impossible to evenly heat the rooms.

"I worked a twelve-hour shift," Sax explained, "I came straight here." She could hear music, and it was loud, coming from upstairs. "Is Quinn here?"

"Yeah, she's upstairs with a friend," Zane explained.

"Anyone I know?" Sax asked, wanting to be involved. She knew the names of all the friends Quinn had in her circle. She knew of their parents, too. Jenner shared so much with her that Sax always felt as if she was in the loop. And she wanted to continue to feel that way.

"I don't know, I didn't ask," Zane said, sounding like the uninvolved father that he was. Zane then invited her to sit down and asked her if she wanted a drink.

Sax wanted to respond *absolutely not*, knowing what had happened the last time they had too much to drink together, but instead she replied, "No, thanks." And she didn't sit down either. She stood about ten feet in front of Zane, who sat down on the arm edge of the burnt orange sofa.

"You called me here because of Quinn," Sax began, wondering if Zane had a change of heart. Maybe he would allow her to share custody, or better. "Is she alright?" Sax wanted to see her before she left there. She wanted to say hi, see her smiling face, and check out who her friend was upstairs in her bedroom with her.

"She's great," he replied. "Could we talk about us for a minute?" Zane suddenly switched gears and what he said sent chills through her.

"There is no us," Sax told him, thankful that the music upstairs was loud. The absolute last thing she wanted was for Quinn to know what happened between her and her father. Sax was trying to put it behind her, and really she almost had, but Zane was resurrecting it.

"We made love..." Zane said, almost sounding as if he had a sensitive side.

"Correction, it was sex," Sax spoke adamantly. She thought of how, yes, she's had sex with men, but *making love*? There was only one man who she had ever made love with. "And it was a mistake," she added, looking him directly in the eyes. "There is no us, and the sooner you accept that, the better off we'll all be."

Sax watched something change in his eyes. He looked hurt, and now angry. "The better off we'll all be?" he asked, coldly. "I will make sure you never see Quinn again!" Zane raised his voice, and again Sax was grateful for the loud music. His words didn't scare her. She was not going to allow him to use her or blackmail her. She wouldn't offer herself, her body, in exchange to keeping the peace for her to be a part of Quinn's life.

"You do not have that power," Sax told him. "Not over me, not over who's in Quinn's life. You don't even have a fucking clue who's upstairs with her right now. You are a piss poor excuse for a father!" Sax spat those words at him, and she wanted to say Quinn would never like him, let alone love him, but she refrained.

Zane was on his feet before Sax realized it. He also had her by the shoulders with his hands. His hands were large and putting pressure on her that was uncomfortable at first, but quickly started to hurt. He moved closer to her and pushed his skinny frame up against her body. Again, she noticed his incredible strength. She was scared, but refused to allow him to see that. "Let go of me," she said to him through clenched teeth. And, Zane did let go, but not before he said, "I will have you again."

As badly as Sax didn't want to leave that house without going upstairs to see Quinn, she knew she had to. She was free of Zane's grip so she stepped quickly over to the door. She opened it, glared back at him, but she never said a word in response to what sounded so much like a threat. Sax seriously wondered if he had ever raped a woman before. What she saw in his eyes was scary enough for her to believe he was capable.

A gust of cold wind hit her in the face as she picked up her pace, ascending the three porch steps. She was looking down at the path she was on when suddenly she heard footsteps in front of her. Sax looked up quickly and saw a young, what she thought to be, Asian man. She opened her mouth, but felt alarmed still so nothing came out.

"Good evening, ma'am," Zimmer said to her. "I didn't mean to startle you."

"That's okay," Sax said, still stepping her way to her car and noticed there was no other vehicle parked alongside of the road.

"Is Mr. Ski, inside?" Zimmer asked, keeping his hands in the pockets of his long, black trench coat with a warm winter lining.

"Um, yes," Sax replied. She didn't like the idea of strangers coming and going in that house while Quinn was there. But this young man did seem harmless. Zimmer kept stepping past Quinn and he was still standing at the door when Sax got into her car and turned the key in the ignition. She didn't wait to see if Zane let him inside. She just checked her car mirrors, and then made a quick U-turn in the middle of the road to get out of there.

Sax turned the heat up and then cracked her driver's side window. Her nerves were shaken. She had to have a cigarette. When she reached for the lighter in her car, she realized her cell phone was missing. She forgot about lighting up as she fumbled through her handbag on the passenger seat. That phone was her lifeline. She felt lost without it. *What if Quinn needed her and wasn't able to contact her?* Sax was wearing dress pants without pockets and again only a heavy sweater with no coat. She suspected where she had left her phone, and she was headed back to the hospital now to retrieve it from her white lab coat.

It took Zimmer a minute to reach for the doorbell. When he and Seth returned to the hotel this evening, Zimmer said he was going to go for a walk. He blamed the heavy pasta dish he had eaten for a late lunch. Seth was relieved to have some time alone. He wanted to drive by the old apartment building where he and Sax had lived together for three years. He contemplated trying to locate her new address as he assumed she was still living in Salem, or at least the local area. They were leaving tomorrow afternoon to drive back to Chicago. If he wanted to see that she had moved on without him, now was the time.

Zane had already gone back downstairs and into his art studio. When he was filled with emotion, he painted. Some of his greatest inspiration had come when he was heartbroken. It happened with Jenner, for years. But, now, he was finally moving on from her. He had to. She was dead. It was Sax Arynn's turn to be the drive behind his next collection.

The music was loud, and Zimmer assumed the doorbell had gone unheard. He knew this was his only chance. They were heading back to Chicago in less than twenty-four hours. He tried the door handle and then pushed the door open. The living room was bright and as he spanned the area he spotted the basement door open near the base of the staircase. He closed the front door and walked toward that open door, leading down to the basement. There was no railing on either side of the steps which were steep and felt rickety beneath his feet. He was wearing black cowboy boots, black denim, a black t-shirt underneath a black long-sleeved v-neck sweater. All of that was covered with his long, black trench coat. Zimmer recognized the familiar scent of paint hanging in the stairwell. He was making his way to the right place, and Zimmer was certain in that art studio he was going to find the man who stole from him.

He turned to the right as soon as he descended the stairs. The wide-open space of that well-lit basement surprised him. The ceilings were at least twelve, or maybe even fifteen-feet tall. There were easels placed everywhere and Zimmer noticed a glass-topped paint table similar to the one he owned. It was used to scrape the dry paint off of the artwork. In the middle of the basement, Zimmer saw him. He was standing with his back to him, in front of a massive easel that had a crank attached to raise and lower the painting. Right now, he had the painting raised to the max, probably twelve foot in the air. It was a portrait, a full body image of a woman. She was beautiful and curvaceous, but Zimmer didn't particularly care about staring at a woman's body. He did, however, take note of her hair. The ash brown color was striking in paint. Her hairdo was cropped short, up to the back of her neckline, and then the full locks on the top of her head were parted wildly and unevenly chic on one side, leaving her long bangs to partially cover her right eye. It never even occurred to Zimmer that he had just passed that very same woman in the dark, outside on the walkway.

He had his hands in both of the deep, front pockets of his trench coat. He felt unusually calm as he stepped closer to the back of the artist in his basement. The music could still be heard coming from upstairs, but otherwise it was silent down there. Zane preferred to work in quiet. He did hear someone behind him though. The heels of the hard cowboy boots on the concrete, even when Zimmer was trying to be quiet, made a slight thumping sound.

Zane spun around and his eyes widened. "What the hell? How did you get in here?" he demanded, and Zimmer didn't act like he was a stranger. He expected Zane Ski to know who he was. Afterall, he was an artist, too. Surely, Zane Ski had wanted to match a face with the collection he had stolen?

"You know exactly who I am," Zimmer spoke, keeping his cool, even though he felt as if his heart was about to beat out of his chest. This confrontation was long-awaited for him. He had played it out in his mind, over and over again. And it never ended well. For Zane Ski.

Zane momentarily considered reaching into the back pocket of his worn, black jeans to retrieve his cell phone to call the police. But, this was just a kid in front of him. Maybe an admirer of his work? He didn't want anyone seeing his art in that basement, not before it was finished. And, it alarmed him that this kid had just walked into his house, and studio, uninvited. "I have no idea who you are," Zane stated.

"I'm an artist," Zimmer told him, "just like you." Zane nodded his head once. "I may be a little green yet, but you obviously saw something in my work as worthy."

"Excuse me?" Zane asked. He, for one semester at Kaskaskia College in Centralia, Illinois, a city only eighteen miles from Salem, taught a beginners art class to collect a paycheck and pay off some bills he had been struggling with. But, teaching was too structured for him. He needed all of the hours in the day, and night, to be able to create. Zane wondered if this kid was one of his students then.

"I specialize in human figures, portraits, still-life, and landscapes," Zimmer began to speak, still standing a great distance away from Zane. "I'm an oil painter. I earned a Masters of Fine Arts in figurative art from the New York Academy of Art."

"Impressive," Zane said, nonchalantly, "but you still have not told me what you're doing here." Zane wanted to get back to his portrait. He was so pleased with how it had turned out so far. Sax Arynn inspired him. Her body was his subject and had been on this massive easel since the night he took her as his own on the hardwood floor upstairs.

"Yes, you were impressed," Zimmer said, keeping only one hand in his trench coat pocket now. "Impressed enough to steal my entire collection." Zane's eyes did not widen, but he felt like his facial expression dropped. This kid, this artist, had tracked him down. He had stolen from him, yes, but Zane was not about to admit it.

"My artwork is my own, thank you," Zane spat at him. "You can see yourself out now."

"Oh, no, I just got here," Zimmer spoke with certainty, "and I'm not leaving until you get what you deserve."

"Excuse me? You are mistaken, and–"

"And what?" Zimmer interrupted him, and before Zane could attempt to get another word in, Zimmer pulled a .357 derringer pistol out of his coat pocket and pointed it at Zane. This time Zane's eyes widened and he took at least three steps back, bumping his shoulder on the immense easel beside him and causing it to rock in place. "I will leave when I want to leave, when I'm through. With you," Zimmer spoke as if he was in a trance. There was a frightening distance in his eyes.

"So you're going to kill me because you think I stole your work?" Zane asked him, as he tried to suppress how scared out of his mind he was.

"No!" Zimmer screamed at him. "No one ever admits they are wrong. Like, my classmates. Oh how I loathed those four years of Forest Park High School." Zane thought of the actual park of the same name in St. Louis and then felt confused. "In the classrooms. The locker rooms. The bathrooms. The parking lot. It never ended. Those fuckers bullied me day in and day out. It did no good for me to tell my parents or the principal. Those goons were never wrong. Never admitted to hurting me. Just like you," Zimmer glared at Zane.

"Look, I'm sorry you've had a rough time, but I'm not those people you are speaking of…" Zane was trying, but he was so weirded out by this kid right now that he couldn't think clearly.

"That's where you are wrong. Dead wrong. I thought I had gotten past the craziness those kinds of people brought to my life. I was accepted by everyone in college and I earned the respect that goes along with the degree. I was on my way. Until you stole from me! You disrespected and mocked me just like they did…" Zimmer's voice cracked and his clammy hand was beginning to shake. His finger was on the gun's trigger, and Zane swallowed hard. *This kid was going to kill him.*

Zane never said a word. He was dumbfounded by what was happening. *What were the chances of stealing artwork from a crazy kid who would track him down and pull a gun on him?* He wasn't going to allow it to end like this. He was not going to be a victim of some lunatic kid. With his large, strong, hands he grabbed ahold of the side of the massive easel beside him and pushed it over, with everything he had. Fear. Adrenaline. Anger at how this could be the end for him. If he allowed it.

The easel came down hard and fast, but Zimmer managed to move just as it slammed to the floor and caught the heel of his boot. He tripped, fell forward and let go of the gun in his hand as he hit the ground hard. The gun slid fast on the concrete floor and Zane stopped it with his own foot. He bent forward and took it into his own hands as he pointed it at a kid who was now back on his feet in front of him.

"Get the hell out of my house!" Zane ordered him.

"Not without doing what I came here for," Zimmer said, almost appearing oblivious to the fact that he was now on the opposite end of the pistol which could put a bullet in him.

Zimmer started to move toward Zane, his steps quickly became a charge. He was going to get his weapon back. He couldn't take back his artwork, but he was there to seek justice his way. Zimmer had that crazed look in his eyes. It all seemed like it was happening in slow motion, and Zane did not hesitate to pull the trigger. It was self defense. He was an intruder.

Chapter 12

Seth was parked in his black Ford Explorer, outside of the apartment building on Manor Street where he and Sax had lived together for three years. He couldn't stay in that hotel room alone after Zimmer went out for a walk. He was in Salem and so close to Sax, he could feel she was still there, still living in that town. He at least wanted to believe that. And now he wanted to see her again. If it was the last thing he did before they left town tomorrow, he wanted to make certain he saw her.

While sitting there, Seth used his cell phone to punch in her name. Again, the white pages led him to the answers he sought. She was still registered under Sax Arynn and their old address on Manor Street remained listed, as well as one new address. He was familiar with the street, he thought, as he shifted his vehicle into drive and made his way to Dietrich.

It was dark, but the street lights lit up a little yellow house on the corner. It didn't look like anyone was home as Seth couldn't see light in the windows. He smiled a little, remembering how yellow was her favorite color. *Pale, not bright,* she would say. He wondered who lived there with her. *A boyfriend? A husband? Maybe children? Her family?*

The ring of his cell phone startled him as he sat idle in his vehicle in the middle of the street, in front of what he believed was Sax's house. He saw Zimmer was calling and he assumed he was back from his walk and at the hotel. He probably wanted to do another drive-by of the old mansion. Seth chuckled to himself at the thought of a kid of twenty-two years old who could pass for eighteen, wanting to stand up to the man who had stolen his paintings. "Hello?" Seth said, with a happy tone in his voice. He enjoyed that kid.

"Pick...me...up," his words were slow and Seth could hear the struggle it was for him to speak.

"Zimmer? What's going on? Are you okay?" The first thing Seth thought of was how there could have been an accident. *God forbid, he was struck by a car as he walked along a dark street.*

"E...ast edge. Hur...ry." Their connection went dead, and Seth slammed his foot hard on the gas pedal. The old mansion was on the east edge of town and now he knew something bad had happened.

Seth drove too fast up and down the dark streets until he reached the old mansion on that dead end. He threw his truck into park in the middle of the street. He saw that familiar white Mustang parked alongside of the curb. And then he looked again. On the street, beside that car, was a person, lying on the road. And it was Zimmer.

Seth flew out of his truck, leaving his door wide open. He met Zimmer on the ground as he fell to his own knees. "What the hell happened?" He looked him over from head to toe as his headlights were shining on them. Zimmer was holding his right hand over his chest and just as he stammered, *sh...shot,* Seth had pulled his hand away and he saw blood. On Zimmer. On his own hand. Zimmer had been shot.

"Oh my God, Oh my God, Oh my God!" Seth panicked before he could think. And then he sprung into action. He took off his coat and applied pressure on the wound. He instructed Zimmer to hold his hand over the coat and push hard. Seth bolted over to his vehicle and opened the passenger door, wide. There was no time to call for an ambulance. He would rush Zimmer to the emergency room himself. Seth wasn't sure how badly Zimmer was hurt, the severity of the gunshot wound, but he was scared out of his mind to know something had happened in that house. And his young friend could have been killed.

✱ ✱ ✱

Sax used her key to enter the lab. That part of the hospital was closed to patients at night, but the lab itself was always active. The rest of the hospital was busy tonight and Sax had just spent the last half an hour talking to one of the maintenance men on the night shift. She enjoyed everyone on staff there. Many of them had become her friends. None like Jenner though, and everyone in that building felt the void of her absence.

Tonight, Rue was working alone in the lab. When Sax opened the door, she looked up. "What brings you back, dear?" Rue asked, only taking her eyes off of what she was testing for a moment.

"My phone. I left it in my lab coat," Sax explained.

"Ahh…that explains the buzzing or vibrating I've been hearing off and on all evening." Rue's focus was back on the vial of blood in front of her and she was using a syringe to place sample drops on the tiny glass square placed under the microscope lens.

"Sorry to interrupt. I'm usually not so careless," Sax said, retrieving her phone from the pocket as her lab coat hung on metal hook near the door. She was relieved to have found it. Rue never looked up or responded to Sax. Rue was dedicated to her career and Sax had seen her in the zone before, but never like this. She felt like she truly was interrupting her. "It seems crazy busy here tonight," Sax made note, and Rue looked up.

"It has been. Lots coming in to the ER," Rue responded, again only taking a moment away from her work for Sax. The emergency room was adjacent to the lab, and Sax knew Rue probably had too many disruptions tonight, so she opted to leave since she now had her phone that she returned for.

She made the motion to step toward the door and Rue kept working. Sax hesitated and then decided not to say goodbye. Rue never noticed as she continued to keep her eyes on what was happening in front of her. Her gloved hands, the blood she had drawn from her own body, the syringe, the microscope. She had to know, and soon she would.

Sax began to walk down the hallway, away from both the lab and the emergency entrance. The lab had to be entered from inside the hospital, but the ER entrance were the two sliding, automatic doors from outside. Her back was to the emergency room door as she moved down the hallway. She heard a ruckus coming in, but this was a hospital, emergencies happen and she rarely ever turned to stare when things weren't calm and collective.

She took at least five or six more steps and she reached the door leading to the outside where she had parked her car in the south side lot. Both of her hands were placed on the metal strip on the door's middle, in position to push it open. And that's when she turned to look back. Nothing made her do it. There were no alarming sounds or even voices. It was just the sight of one man carrying another person, and Sax couldn't tell if it was a female or male who was being brought into the ER. All she saw was the back of a man, carrying someone, in a hurry.

It had happened to her many times before, but not so much anymore. There was that rush of emotion. That flushed feeling of all the blood making its way to her face. Her heartbeat quickened and she felt a familiar pain stab her to her very core whenever she *thought* she saw him. Same height. Hair. Build. It wasn't him, but it always seemed like it could have been. Sax just stood there, both of her hands were still on the door, with her body twisted around to look back. She remained frozen in that awkward position after that man turned the corner into the emergency room.

There was no possible way it was Seth Moss. He had been away from Salem for years. And was never coming back. Sax told herself so three times as she walked to her car and was able to begin breathing again.

Seth waited forty-five minutes to be told that Zimmer had a flesh wound near his shoulder. The bullet, embedded in muscle, did no damage to his bones or vital organs. The bullet was removed by the ER physician and Zimmer was given eight stitches. He would be fine, but the police would be asking questions very soon. It was protocol when a patient was brought in with a gunshot wound. Seth hoped the police would go straight to Zimmer, because that was exactly what he intended to do to get answers.

He was told he could see his friend, so Seth followed the nurse back to the compact room behind the curtain. Zimmer was lying on a gurney, wearing a hospital gown, and covered up to his waist. His eyes were closed, but he opened them as he heard Seth approach his bedside.

"Looks like I'm gonna live," Zimmer smirked, but winced from the intense pain he continued to have in his shoulder. His pain medicine had yet to kick in. He was pale, weak, but feeling stronger emotionally just knowing he had survived a bullet. Only tough guys did things like that. And Zimmer had never seen himself as tough.

"Tell me what happened," Seth said, sounding demanding.

"I confronted him. He was angry. He pulled a gun on me and fired." Zimmer spoke in no uncertain terms. Sometimes even liars believed themselves.

"Holy shit, Zimmer! You could have been killed! You have no idea what people are capable of! Screw the paintings! Yes, you took a loss when that thief stole all of your artwork, but you could have lost your life tonight! Nothing is worth that! Do you hear me?"

"I hear how much you care," Zimmer replied. "Thank you."

"You're welcome," Seth smiled at him, still feeling so much relief from knowing he was going to be just fine. "Any idea when you can get out of here?"

"I hope before the police show up," Zimmer stated.

"What? Why would you not want to press charges against that crazed fucker who shot you?" Seth was confused and still reeling from how they made this trip together, but he could have been going back to Chicago alone. All because Zimmer wanted to confront an art thief, and he wanted to find closure knowing Sax Arynn was happy.

"I just want to forget, you know?" Zimmer said, succeeding at coming across as innocent and Seth nodded his head.

"I get that, I really do," he told him, "but you still have to talk to the police. They need your story. Whether you press charges or not will be your decision. But, if you ask me, that's your ticket to nailing Zane Ski for stealing your artwork."

Zimmer only nodded his head this time, and then the pain medicine began to take affect and he closed his eyes for awhile.

Seth sat down in a chair against the wall and tried to get some rest, too. He was told by an ER nurse that this would be Zimmer's room until the morning. There were no vacant rooms on the hospital floor, so they were cramming admitted patients into the ER cubicles as needed.

✶ ✶ ✶

Sax hardly slept at all after she finally made it home from the hospital. There was just too much on her mind. Zane was acting lovesick and borderline crazy. Now, more than ever, she didn't want Quinn in that house with him. And then there was that man in the hospital, rushing into the ER. She never saw his face. Just a view of his body from behind. *Would she ever get over Seth Moss?* After nearly seven years, she doubted she ever would.

Two hours before she was supposed to be at work, Sax was walking through the lab door already at six o'clock. She didn't have to unlock the door this time. Patients were already coming in for blood withdrawal and two other medical technicians were on staff for that. Sax was going to spend most of her work day in the lab.

While she was slipping on her white lab coat, a Salem Police Officer was walking into the emergency room across the hall, asking for the patient who was brought in with a gunshot wound last night.

Seth had been sitting in that same chair against the wall, talking to Zimmer, who was awake and in pain again, when the middle-aged, heavy-set and balding officer entered and asked him to leave the room while he spoke to *Mr. Jason Zimmer.*

Seth wasn't sure where to go, so he started walking the hallway in between the lab and the ER. He found a restroom. After he relieved his bladder, he stood by the sink and splashed some water on his face. It had been a long, too eventful night. He was ready to go back home, to Chicago. As strangely comfortable as he did feel being back in Salem, he knew he no longer belonged there. He wished though that he could have seen her. Just once more.

Sax was called out of the lab and into the ER to withdraw blood from a patient. She was carrying a tray with three complete vials of blood as she walked down the hallway, en route to the lab. She was wearing black fitted dress pants with ballet flats, and underneath her white lab coat she wore a coral cowl neck sweater. As she was walking, Sax spotted another medical technician. "Hey Christy, can you do me a favor?" Sax asked her, and she nodded. "Take this tray back to the lab. It's ready to go, labels and all. I'm going to the courtyard for a smoke."

After Sax passed the restrooms on her left, Seth walked out. He looked before he stepped out into the hallway and that's when he saw her. She was twenty or thirty feet away from him.

It was her shape, that body. Her walk. The color of her hair, but the short, sassy style was different. He thought about her last night as he tried to sleep in the ER. He wondered if she still worked there, in that hospital. He pondered the chances of running into her. Now, he saw her, but only from behind. Still, it was her. He knew for sure. The rush of emotions over-whelmed him more than he expected. *How could he have walked away from a woman like her? Temporary insanity,* he told himself. And then he followed her.

She ended up in the courtyard. *She still smoked,* he thought, *and so did he.* Seth watched her light up. They were both smart, healthy people with fit bodies, but neither one of them could kick their addiction to nicotine. He stood back, hidden in the doorway, to ensure she would not see him.

As soon as Zimmer was released from the hospital, they were going to check out of their room at the Salem Inn and drive back to Chicago. *It was now or never. Maybe he should just say hi?*

Hi? After all these years? After leaving her? Giving up on them? All those times he ignored her messages. How could she ever even want to lay eyes on him, much less talk to him?

But, if he didn't walk out there, into that courtyard right now, would he really want another regret to take back to Chicago with him?

Chapter 13

Sax was back in the lab, and had just sat down on the stool in front of the microscope she preferred to use when Rue walked in. There was an awkward silence in the room, which was never the case when Rue was around.

"Good morning," Sax said to her, noticing how she seemed to be in her own little world. And that was unlike Rue, too. She was always sticking her nose into everyone else's world.

"Morning, honey," Rue replied.

"So I'm hearing a gunshot victim was brought into the ER last night," Sax spoke entirely out of character. This would be right up Rue's alley. Her cup of tea. She loved gossip. "Any idea what happened in our sleepy little town?"

Rue looked at Sax and all but shook her head. "What's gotten into you?" she asked her.

"Just surprised to hear that, and curious about what the heck happened!" Sax answered as she wondered if Rue would confide in her about what was bothering her.

"I have no idea," Rue replied. "What does it matter anyway? We're all going to die of something. I think I'd rather be shot, let it be quick though. I don't want to suffer much. Even a car accident would work." Rue was rambling now, and Sax's face fell. "Oh, honey, I'm sorry. Me and my big mouth. I didn't mean to–"

"Bring up the fact that my dearest friend in the whole universe was killed in a car accident?" Sax interjected. "I don't need any reminders. It's always there." Sax wasn't sure what was going on with Rue, but at this point she was done talking to her. Everyone had their own pain. *Just carry it and move on.* Sax's cynicism always escalated around Rue.

"I heard it was a young man, twenty-two years old," Rue began to answer Sax's question from earlier. "Just a flesh wound. He'll be out of here today or tonight." Sax nodded her head and wondered if he was the one carried in last night. The image of who she thought she saw, from a hallway's distance away, was still with her.

Across the hall, in the ER, Seth was back in the compact exam room which he hoped would not be Zimmer's for too much longer. While he was watching Sax in the courtyard, Zimmer had sent him a text. The police officer had taken his statement and told him he could not leave Salem until after Zane Ski's statement was obtained as well. Zimmer panicked, but feigned calm with Seth. "I have to stay in town until after the police question Zane Ski," he told Seth.

"How long will that be?" Seth asked, hoping he would be back in Chicago and at work on Monday morning.

"Like twenty-four hours or something," Zimmer answered. "I'm sure we can still leave by Sunday night." Seth nodded his head and accepted more of Zimmer's words as the truth. He had no reason not to believe him. But, he was lying. Nothing was said about twenty-four hours. The police never gave him a time frame. The officer only said, *don't leave town.* But, Zimmer had one more thing to take care of and then he and Seth could be on their way back home.

When the same officer from the Salem Police Department showed up on the front porch of the old mansion, Zane wasn't surprised. He saw that crazed kid run out of his basement with a bullet in his shoulder. He knew he would survive, but not without medical treatment which meant the police would learn someone took a bullet in that old mansion on the east edge of town. And Zane was ready for his side of the story.

"Hello officer," Zane said, answering the door in black jeans, boots, and a clean white t-shirt.

"We received a report of a shooting here last night," the middle-aged, heavy-set bald officer spoke, "and I do have a few questions for you."

Zane invited the officer inside, but he chose not to sit down. He just started asking questions.

"What happened here last night?"the officer asked Zane.

"I had an intruder," Zane told him, fidgeting with his long ponytail, and the officer stared at the tattoos that covered both of his forearms.

"A break in?" the officer asked, with his pen and notepad in hand. With today's technology, Zane thought of that as odd.

"No. My doors are rarely locked," Zane explained. "It was evening and I was downstairs in my studio. I turned around and that punk was standing there. He accused me of stealing his art. Everyone always wants a piece of success. I own what I create. Anyway, he was angry and talking out of his head about being bullied as a teenager and before I knew it, he pulled a gun on me."

"He pulled a gun on you?" the officer asked, needing clarification.

"Yes, and he was going to use it," Zane spoke, honestly. "I took action to try to save my own life. I pushed a twelve-foot easel over on him. It caught his leg, he fell and the gun ended up on the concrete floor. I grabbed it, aimed, and fired. He was an intruder, and I shot him in self defense." The officer was thinking how there were always two sides to every story. One man's word against another's. "Here," Zane said, reaching behind his back to retrieve the handgun he had wedged in between his belt and his pants. "Run a check. This is not my gun."

Zimmer didn't know it, but his release from the hospital was being prolonged. The ER physician who treated the gunshot victim was instructed not to release the patient until further notice.

The buzz was all over the hospital now, but Seth wasn't there to be in the know. He had gone back to the hotel to pack his things and Zimmer's. Their plan was to leave for Chicago as soon as possible. Seth would drive and Zimmer could rest. There was nothing keeping either of them in Salem.

A few hours later, Seth was driving back to the hospital and he thought about seeing Sax in the courtyard. It was all he had thought about since he saw her. She looked different, yet still the same. It was still her, with spunk and flare, and attitude. *God, how he missed her. And what a fool he had been to let her go.*

Zimmer was upset, sitting up in bed with a scowl on his face, when Seth walked in. "Now what? You should be happy to be getting out of here soon," Seth said, carrying in a bag with a change of clothes in it for Zimmer and he put it down on the foot end of the bed, near Zimmer's covered legs.

"That's just it, no doctor, no release yet," Zimmer complained. He wasn't just restless, he was nervous. He lied to the police and he wanted to get the hell out of that city before the truth about what occurred in Zane Ski's basement surfaced.

"Sit tight, this is a busy place. We'll get you out of here and on the road soon," Seth reassured him and realized he sounded like a father figure sometimes when he was around Zimmer. While he was a man of twenty-two, he just seemed like he needed guidance. Seth didn't mind taking him under his wing. *He was a good kid.* "Have you eaten? I need to grab something from the cafeteria before I pass out," Seth told him.

"You go ahead, I'm not hungry," Zimmer said. As Seth began to leave the room, Zimmer stopped him.

"Hey, um, I just want to say thanks again. I know this trip isn't at all like you expected. I mean, you never got to track her down...and get your closure." Zimmer was being sincere. And he also felt guilty for dragging a good man who had quickly become a loyal friend, into this mess. He did realize that his actions were going to have consequences, sooner or later.

"No thanks necessary," Seth said, reaching the doorway and pushing open the door. "And don't you worry about me. I've done alright, and I'll be alright."

When Seth left, he needed a smoke. Sometimes, before he ate, he had to have a nicotine fix. Sax was the same way. Only, for her, that cigarette often times ended up replacing her meal. She hadn't had much of an appetite since Jenner died. She would crave something to eat, but after a few bites she was no longer hungry or interested enough to finish.

There were two entrances to the outside courtyard. Seth had found the one closest to the lab and emergency room. Sax was on the opposite side of the hospital and had just withdrawn blood from a patient in a private room. She left the samples at the nurse's station with the intent of coming right back to retrieve them after she had a smoke outside in the courtyard.

Both doors on opposite ends of the courtyard were opened at the same time. Both of them were fumbling for their cigarette and lighter. Looking down. Digging into a pocket. Using a hand to block the wind for the end of the cigarette to catch fire. Three steps forward on the north end. Three steps forward on the south end. Both oblivious to not being alone out there.

Until, in sync, Sax raised her head, and so did Seth. *It was her. It was him.* It was as if no time had passed. And too much time had passed. *How could it feel like both?* Sax froze. It was chilly out there, not freezing, but suddenly she felt frozen. Her lips lost hold of the newly lit cigarette and it fell to the ground, at her feet. She never bent down to retrieve it. And, Seth's cigarette never did light. He took it out of his mouth and held it in his hand. She wasn't moving. But, he was.

He walked toward her, and she never took her eyes off of him. When he reached her, he stopped about eight feet away. "Sax…" *Did he have to say her name? Did it have to sound just the same?* He looked the same too. Same haircut. Same fit, tight, broad chest. Seven years may have shown on his face a tad. He looked less baby-faced and more manly. *Why was she even taking note of that?*

"It's been a long damn time," he said, feeling as if he was holding his breath for a response from her. She looked even more beautiful, up close now, than he remembered. Her hair styled that way was taking some getting used to. But, he liked it. When they were together, she had long hair. He remembered her tying it up in a knot on top of her head on lazy weekend mornings and sometimes she would leave it that way all day long. Time and again, he used to take it out and watch it fall onto her shoulders. That always led to kissing her, touching her, and never being able to stop. "How are you?"

"What are you doing here?" Sax managed to string together those words when her mind and body felt so incredibly frazzled right now.

"Long story, but a friend of mine was admitted last night," he began.

"I don't mean here," she interrupted, referring to the hospital. "I mean in Salem." *Why, after all this time, six years and ten months, had he come back? And, why was she giving him the time of day? He didn't deserve her attention.*

"I'm here as a favor for a friend," he replied, "and to be honest, I wanted to look you up…" There, he had said it.

"Look me up?" she asked, feeling sarcastic and pissed off from the pain. "As in call up an old friend to have a drink to rehash the good times and get caught up on life as it is now?" Seth was expecting this from her. In fact, he had expected nothing less. The shock had worn off, somewhat, and now she was angry. He had the advantage of seeing her first, yesterday. He was oblivious to the fact that she thought she had seen him as well last night. Deep down, she had known, that time, it was really him. She just hadn't allowed herself to face it.

"I think we could both use a drink right about now," Seth tried to smile, but Sax wasn't amused. Her white lab coat was buttoned, but blowing open at the bottom each time the wind picked up. She noticed him in his tight jeans, Doc Martin brown tie shoes, and blue, snug fitting Chicago Bears quarter-zip.

"Did I drive you to drink, Seth?" she asked him, she said his name, and it still felt good to feel it roll off her tongue. She could have cursed herself for feeling that way. He looked confused by her words, but he did understand her being so upset with him. Even after all these years. "Three years of just not being where you wanted to be. Three years of coming home to me. Here I was thinking this is it. This man completes me. I have a career that I enjoy and it pays the bills, but *my life* was you. My heart, my soul, my being, was you." Seth only listened. She had never spoken like that to him. Or at least he had not heard her, if she had. Her honesty right now touched him. "And, you, in turn, must have felt like love was some sort of prison."

"That's not true," he cut her off.

"No?" she asked, awaiting an explanation then.

"No," he answered. "I was out of my mind. Young and stupid." Sax did not want to hear that from him. Not now. Not ever. *It was too late. There was too much anger. Too much pain.* "I'm sorry," he said to her, sincerely. Sax could see in his eyes how regretful he was. She forced herself not to pay attention to that. He never had taken notice of her when she was hurting and resorted to begging him not to give up on them. The thought of that embarrassed her now. She just had not known how to let go then. She still didn't, but for the first time in several years, she felt strong enough to hold her own and not allow him to see her vulnerability for him. For them. For who they used to be together. She had never come close to finding a love like they shared. But, again, she reminded herself how one-sided their love was. It never felt like it was one-sided. She hadn't picked up on any signs. But, it was. He left, so it was.

Sax never responded to his apology, so he spoke again. "I'm sure my words mean nothing to you now, but just know that I mean it. I know how wrong I was."

"Stop it," Sax said to him. "Just stop."

"I want to know that you're happy," he said to her. "I need–"

"You need?" she interjected. "It was about *your need.* Your need to leave. To be free of me. Do your friend that favor in this town and then go back to Chicago or wherever it is that you felt called to be alone, or with someone better." Sax didn't mean to, but she looked for a wedding ring on his left hand, fourth finger. Nothing. It didn't mean he wasn't committed.

"There is no one better," he told her. He allowed her to be angry with him. She had every right to be. He was in disbelief that she had given him this much of her time already. He knew it was coming to an end. It's what she did when she boiled over. She stood her ground only for so long, and then she walked away. She was the toughest woman he had ever known, but sometimes she could only handle so much. She had been through too much, and Seth only knew half of it. He had no idea of her pain in recent months.

Sax swallowed hard. Those words would not melt her. His eyes piercing hers would not sway her. Forgiveness was not in the cards for them. Not for her. "I have to get back to work," she said, beginning to turn on the heels of her black ballet flats that she was wearing without socks. She never wore a coat, she didn't wear socks when she should have. Those things mirrored her in ways she never realized. The cold didn't force her to wear a coat. And neither did wearing socks in all shoes. Sax Arynn made up her own rules. No one told her what to do, or how to feel. But, she was struggling right now with how she felt about this man. This man who would always have a hold on her, and her heart, no matter how hard she tried not to let him.

"Does he love you?" Seth's words forced her to turn back around. "Is he worthy of a woman like you? Does he know that he'll never find anyone else to measure up? Smart. Sassy. Spunky. Tough on that beautiful exterior, but a marshmallow inside. Does he appreciate every ounce of that?"

"Who are you talking about?" Sax asked him, trying to sound annoyed. She knew all of those amazing compliments were meant for her. And she also knew Seth implied that she had a new man in her life. He thought someone else had taken his place. *Little did he know.*

"I hope you've found someone to love you, someone you deserve," he said, feeling like he was ripping out his own heart. He wasn't being entirely truthful. Yes, she deserved to be handed the sun, the moon, and the stars. But, he wanted to be the one to give those things to her. But, he knew, he had his chance. And he had thrown it away.

"I have," Sax lied, and then she turned and walked away. And, this time, Seth never stopped her.

Chapter 14

Sax rushed straight into the lab. She didn't look up at anyone she met in the hallway along the way, even if they greeted her. It took everything she had not to fall apart right then and there when she turned and walked away from Seth. Her hands were shaking and her mind was spinning. She slammed the lab door behind her and was relieved to see it was empty. Her back was up against the closed door and her face was instantly in her hands. And the tears could wait no more. She stood there and openly cried for what that man had done to her. To them. And for how he still made her feel.

She thought she was alone and continued to come undone. But, in the storage closet, in the far corner of the room, was Rue. She just stayed in there and watched Sax. *That poor girl*, she thought. And to Rue, she was just a girl. She had her entire life ahead of her yet, but so much thus far had been coated in pain. It was practically all she knew, and that is why Rue felt compelled to help her.

Rue walked out of the storage closet and Sax immediately tried to pull herself together. "I thought I was alone," she said, wiping the tears off of her face, and wishing she had a tissue in her lab coat pocket to blow her nose. She walked over to a side table, pushed up against the wall, and found a box of tissues. She kept her back to Rue as she dabbed her eyes with it and then blew her nose. Rue then walked up directly behind her and Sax could feel her thick arms around her. She held her, just like that, for a few minutes as Sax started to sob again. "Let it out, honey. Release those bottled up emotions. You have to. You need to." Sax realized that Rue believed she was mourning Jenner, and she was. But, right now, she was mourning a relationship that could never be. And *that* hurt like hell all over again.

When Sax finally stopped crying, Rue let go of her. "I'm sorry," Sax spoke softly as she regained her composure.

"Don't be. It's human to cry. You're human, you're not superwoman." Sax thought Rue's eyes looked red as well, as if she too had been upset. Could have been why she had stepped into the supply closet.

"How about you? Are you okay?" Sax recognized how she had not been acting like herself the past couple of days.

"I'm just worried about you," Rue answered, but Sax didn't believe her. *Maybe they both were a little alike afterall?* Neither one of them wanted to tell the other what was really going on.

✳ ✳ ✳

Seth never went back to Zimmer's room. He just entered the hospital again from the courtyard and then walked through the nearest hallway to bring him to any exit. He took the first one he could find and got out of that building. He walked around the parking lot, trying to figure out where he was parked. Once he found his SUV, after walking in circles for at least five minutes, he got inside and just sat behind the wheel, staring. And thinking. What was really in Chicago for him? *A damn good job. A few good friends. A nice penthouse apartment.* But, none of it meant to him what that woman had, and still did. He cursed himself, now more than ever, for being young and stupid, and a believer in bigger and better of everything awaiting him outside of Salem. None of it mattered to him now. And he didn't want to believe it was too late. He wanted to know more about Sax's life now. There was no ring on her finger either.

Seth picked up his phone and prepared to send Zimmer a text. He thought for a moment and then he compiled his message. *Let me know when you are released and I will be back. We are not leaving Salem just yet. I need a few more days.*

Zimmer responded, *okay*. But, that's not what he was thinking. He was beginning to panic, and when he panicked he always made rash decisions.

Chapter 15

Quinn had her feet, in sandy-brown Ugg boots, up on Sax's pale yellow couch. When Sax walked into the living room from her bedroom, she smiled. That was what life was about for her now. Seeing Quinn making herself at home with her. They were squeezing in some time together after school and before Sax had to work the night shift at the hospital. There was an overload of lab work and Rue had asked her to help her catch up, for overtime pay.

"Do you want to eat something before you have to go back to your dad's?" Sax asked her, standing beside the sofa and Quinn was texting someone on her phone.

"Yeah, if you do," Quinn replied, "but, can you drop me off at a friend's house instead?"

"You don't want to go home?" Sax asked, feeling guilty for not being able to do more to keep Quinn with her permanently.

"I hate it there," she responded.

"I know, sweetie, and I'm sorry," Sax told her. She never wanted to make promises to Quinn that she could not keep, but Sax had already vowed to herself to make it happen. She wanted Quinn in her life, in her home, and away from Zane. "Maybe make the time pass by having friends over?" Sax suggested.

"I would be embarrassed to have my friends there," she admitted, and Sax was so amazed how this girl who didn't always openly communicate was now so comfortable talking and sharing her thoughts. Sax felt closer to her than ever now. "The man I'm supposed to call my dad is just weird. Sometimes I think he's trying with me, and other times he's so lost in his art that he doesn't even know I'm there."

Sax had seen both sides of what Quinn described. "So, wait, you've never had friends in?" Sax was puzzled, remembering the loud music and Zane's mention of her having a friend upstairs with her in her bedroom.

"Nope," Quinn stated.

"I stopped by recently to talk to your dad…about something," Sax paused, "and the music was loud, coming from your bedroom. Zane said you had a friend up there?"

Quinn smiled, and Sax held her breath. *Please God, no boys. Not yet. Damn you, Jenner for leaving me to deal with this. A preteen on the verge of wild teenage years.* But, it wasn't what Sax feared. "I tell him that sometimes. He never checks up on me anyway," Quinn began, and Sax's eyes widened. "I leave. I go to Emily's or Lauren's. It works every time. When I return, I turn the music off."

"Please be cautious walking alone on the streets at night," Sax told her, well aware that neither of her friends lived close by. She chose her words carefully. She wanted Quinn to know that she trusted her. "If you ever need a ride, call me. I mean it. There are some crazies out there." Quinn nodded her head. Sax wanted to tell her never to sneak out again, but she didn't. She wasn't in a position to order her or forbid her. She only wanted to take care of her and keep her safe. And, she didn't blame Quinn for not wanting to spend time in that house.

As the two of them were discussing what they could eat for dinner, Sax's doorbell rang. "Well I'll see who's here," she said, turning around from standing near Quinn on the sofa. Sax was already dressed for work, but since she was taking the night shift she was wearing skinny dark denim, a black ribbed turtle neck sweater, and high dark brown boots. She was partial to the contrast of wearing black and brown together. Her hair was longer and fuller on top, and she was getting close to being in need of a haircut again. She found herself brushing it away more often from hanging over her right eye. She looked chic and shapely in her jeans and Quinn smiled at her as she walked toward the door. Quinn always did think Sax defined *cool*.

Sax usually peered through the narrow window to the right of her front door, before unlocking and pulling the door open. But this time, she just opened it. And, when she did, she felt her face flush. It was Seth.

"Hi, what are you doing here?" she asked him as he stood there in tight denim, tennis shoes, and more Chicago Bears apparel. This time it was a blue hoodie. Quinn heard Sax's words and she immediately sat upright on the sofa to see who was at the door. Sax had attitude and could be a sarcastic and downright bitchy to people, and it always made Quinn chuckle. Jenner had tried to protect her from the cussing, the smoking, and that attitude, but finally she just gave up. It was who Sax was, and they both loved her.

"I don't know, exactly," Seth answered, truthfully, as he stuffed both of his hands into his front jean pockets. The wind was blustery and downright cold. "I looked you up. I drove by. And now I'm standing at your front door, freezing and hoping you will invite me inside."

"Now's not a good time," Sax told him, feeling like she was being as polite as she could with Quinn present. What she would like to have done was slammed the door and lock it again. Dead bolt it, too. That's what he had done. Seth closed the door on her. On them. On their life together. And a part of Sax wanted to hate him with every ounce of her being. But, she didn't.

"Please?" he asked, and Sax looked back at Quinn who was staring at both of them from the sofa.

"Come in," Sax muttered under her breath as she stepped back and opened the door wider. Her tone was a cross between defeat and disgust.

As soon as he stepped inside, Seth noticed Quinn. "Oh, hi," he said to her and he knew by her age that she could not be Sax's daughter. Then he wondered if Sax had a husband there, maybe she was his daughter.

"Hi, I'm Quinn," Quinn offered, waving from the sofa, which she no longer had her boots resting on.

"Hi Quinn, I'm Seth," he said in return, and Sax noticed his genuine smile. It was always so infectious. Some things never changed.

"Quinn, this is someone I used to know. He lives in Chicago now, right?" Sax looked at Seth for accuracy.

"Yes, I do," he said, as he waited to hear what Sax's relationship to this girl was.

"Quinn is my best friend's daughter," Sax explained. She noticed how she naturally spoke of Jenner as if she was still her best friend and still alive.

"Oh I see," Seth said, wondering where her best friend was now and even more importantly, who she was. Friends came and went, but he didn't remember a close friend of Sax's having a daughter named Quinn.

"I'm going in your bedroom to call Emily, to make plans for later," Quinn told Sax, knowing she needed some time alone with her old friend. Jenner had told her the story of Seth Moss and how he had broken Sax's heart. Quinn couldn't believe he was there, and she could tell Sax was rattled. She also noticed something in her eyes and her mannerisms, and she believed now what her mother had told her when she was old enough to understand a little about love and how adults sometimes had complicated relationships. Jenner had described *Seth as being the love of Sax's life. The one that got away.*

When Quinn was out of the room, Sax spoke first. "You should not have come here. This is my home. My private life." She wanted to say *it's none of your business*, but she refrained. He should have taken the hint from what she had already said.

"I know that," he told her, "but I didn't want to leave things as we had in the courtyard."

Sax looked both confused and miffed at him, on purpose. "How should we have reacted to seeing each other after almost seven years, considering we didn't end on the best note?"

"Exactly," he agreed, with a crooked smile. "I just wanted to know more about you, your life, and how you really are doing…"

"Why does it matter now?" Sax all but spat at him.

"I don't know, but it does," he told her.

"My life is just that, mine. You are no longer a part of it, and you wanted it to be that way. I can't be your friend, if that's what you're asking." Sax felt so flustered she wasn't even certain if her words were coming out and making sense right now.

Seth shook his head, appearing to be in agreement. "For a moment I thought you had a daughter, just now, but she'd have to be younger."

"Quinn is like a daughter to me," she admitted.

"Her mother must mean a lot to you. Although I know how you love big and take care of your own. Do I know her? Is she from here?" Seth was curious.

"She was from here," Sax answered.

"And she's not anymore?" Seth asked, awaiting more details.

"She died in a car accident a few months ago," Sax said, wondering why she was going there. Why he made her feel like she could talk to him, despite everything.

"How awful," Seth responded, sincerely. "So, are you raising her?"

"I'd like to be," Sax answered, "but, no. She is just now getting to know her birth father. She lives with him."

"That big heart of yours is admirable," Seth said to her, and he meant it. He was touched by how she wanted to be there for her best friend's child.

"It's not all that admirable," she said, feeling cynical again. "It's been broken too many times." Seth was familiar with her pain. Sax's parents died when she was eighteen years old. She had just graduated from high school, and lost them both when their home burned to the ground after an electrical fire. Their existing smoke alarms had expired batteries in them and were never given the chance to sound. It was too late when Sax's parents woke up. The firemen had found them in the hallway, and it was assumed they were trying to escape but the fire had trapped them and the smoke became too much. Sax had been on an overnight camping trip with the graduating seniors in her class. From that night on, she was on her own. Seth also knew he was to blame for additional heart break in Sax's life. And now he felt terrible, knowing her best friend had left her, too. Sax was a tough soul, but he wondered how much more she would be expected to take.

"I know," he agreed with her. "That's why I asked if you've found someone to appreciate all that you are." Sax recalled lying to him in the courtyard, and now she wondered if she could keep it up. *What did it matter? He was going back to Chicago anyways.*

"Your sudden interest in my personal life is weird," she told him, and he laughed.

"Yeah, I guess it does seem weird," he admitted. "I think it's more about closure."

"Why do *you* need closure?" she asked him, because they were both well aware of how and why their relationship ended. He wanted out. He was looking for a change.

"I left this sleepy little town looking for it all, or at least more," he started to explain. "In a big, exciting city I found a career that suited me and flourished year after year. I live in a penthouse that's crazy expensive and just awesome. I've met some wonderful people who I've created lasting friendships with. And I've dated, some…" he paused, "but I haven't found the one." Sax only stared at him, and he spoke again. "Because I had her. I was young and stupid and naïve and any other negative adjective that you want to throw in there, I'll take." Seth took one step toward her, and Sax backed up. They were still standing very close to the front door.

"I don't know what you expect me to say to you right now," she said to him. "I have to get Quinn some dinner, and I have to go to work tonight."

"I understand," he said, knowing he should leave, but not wanting to. "Maybe we could meet at the hospital during your break. For coffee? Or a smoke?"

"Seth," she said his name and it happened to her again. That feeling. But, she quickly pushed *that feeling* away. Out of her mind. But, it wouldn't budge from her heart. It never had. "Just go."

He did leave then, but he planned to see her later as he would be under the same roof with her again when Zimmer was released from the hospital tonight. Sax didn't watch out of the window when he left. She just stood there with her back up against the closed door, thinking how it had taken *some nerve* for him to come there, to her home. But, then again, the comfort level between the two of them had always been effortless.

✳ ✳ ✳

The police had gathered very little information on Jason Zimmer. The .357 derringer pistol was traced to a pawn shop in Chicago. Zimmer did walk into Zane Ski's old mansion uninvited, but he had not broken in. Zimmer was also the man who ended up taking a bullet. There were no charges that could be brought against him. No further evidence or a background of crimes of any sort to warrant further questioning. Zane Ski had wanted him arrested, but that wasn't happening. Zimmer had hoped Zane Ski would pay for attempting to kill him after his own attempt to kill Zane was thwarted. Zimmer had too much time to over think while lying in that hospital bed. Soon, Seth would be back and he would be released. They planned to spend one more night in the hotel before the men from Chicago would go back home within the next twenty-four hours. Zimmer was ready, but now Seth was not.

Chapter 16

Rue seemed back to her old self, in high spirits, as Sax worked in the lab with her. Sax was compliant with keeping the conversation going about whatever Rue brought up, because she didn't want to dwell on seeing Seth again.

"So did you hear our gunshot victim is finally being released tonight?" Rue asked Sax as they were both perched on stools on opposite ends of the lab.

"No, actually I haven't paid much attention to that story," Sax said, wondering if that was indeed the patient Seth had brought in. It had to be. "Has anyone been arrested?"

"No idea. The nurses in the ER said the patient didn't talk much, only to his friend who brought him in when he was shot and visited him quite a bit," Rue stated.

The subject was dropped after that, and Sax started to open up about what was on her mind. "Can I ask you something personal, Rue?"

"Anything, honey. I'm pretty much an open book." Rue winked at her from across their glass-top lab tables.

"Have you ever had someone in your life who didn't stay, for one reason or another, and you just could never seem to find a way to let go of them? No matter how hard you tried?" Sax was revealing something so personal about herself right now she felt frightened and started to rethink the mention of it.

"Oh yes," Rue replied. "The father of my firstborn son."

Sax looked surprised. She knew Rue was married and her husband had died nine years ago after having a massive heart attack. Rue was now in her mid-sixties and at the time she became a widow, she was only fifty-six. Her husband was the same age when he died. Sax thought they shared two sons and one daughter. "I thought you had three children with Ron?" Sax asked her.

"I raised three children with my Ronnie," Rue spoke quietly. "When I got pregnant with my first son, I was infatuated with a man a decade older than me. We had a brief affair."

"An affair?" Sax asked, realizing she meant she was married to Ron at the time.

"My first year of marriage, I cheated on my husband. He never knew," Rue told Sax, not caring if she wanted to judge her now, all these years later. "I passed my baby off as Ron's and we shared a wonderful life together, with two more children."

"Really?" Sax asked, seriously not believing this older woman had *a past.*

"For real, honey," Rue replied. "I knew a man like the one I fell for would never be a good father to my baby. He didn't want me for more than what we sneaked around to do together. I knew the kind of man I married and I do not live with regret. I have, however, lived with what you just asked me about. I have never been able to let that man go. He's been a part of my heart for forty years. I see so much of him in my oldest son, too. So, to answer your question, yes, I have someone's memory very much alive in my soul. Letting go never happened."

"Who else knows about this, your secret?" Sax was still trying to process all of it.

"You," Rue replied with a crooked grin.

"You have never told anyone until just now? Me?" Sax's mouth fell open.

"That's correct," Rue replied. "I had a marriage to protect and a family to keep intact. No one needs to know now either."

"I suppose you're right," Sax said, respecting Rue for her decision in an odd way. She did what she had to do.

"This isn't a secret, but I'm going to share something else with you," Rue began talking again. "I was diagnosed with leukemia after I had my first baby. Ron was my strength throughout that struggle. Before I agreed to treatment, I had my eggs frozen to ensure that I could have more children. Ron deserved that, and I knew why more than anyone. When my cancer went into remission, I had two babies one year apart."

"I had no idea, Rue," Sax said, feeling like she really didn't know this woman at all. She always believed she was catty, nosy, and just old.

"I don't broadcast it, but people know. I'm sure some remember me being sick," Rue stated, with a solemn look on her face.

"But, you beat that awful disease!" Sax said, now sounding like her biggest cheerleader.

"For many, many years, yes," Rue said to her. "But, now, it has come back. I have leukemia again." Sax's face fell. "You walked in on me doing my own diagnostic blood work right here in this lab."

"Oh my God, no," Sax finally spoke. "If you beat it once, you will again, right?" Sax suddenly felt like crying, but she wanted to be there for this woman who she was just now getting to know, for real.

"No way will I put myself through that battle again," Rue said, adamantly. "I did it once because I was young and had so much living ahead that I wanted to do. Not now. My husband is gone, my children are grown, and my grandchildren aren't that little anymore. I'm not really needed all that much, so if it's time for me to go, then so be it."

From across the room, Sax could see the tears in Rue's eyes. She had not moved the entire time she was listening to Rue tell her story, including a secret no one ever knew. Sax was now on her feet and moving toward Rue. Rue remained seated on her stool as Sax enveloped her into her arms. Rue cried and Sax held her for the longest time with a lump in her throat that hurt like hell. She was going to lose yet another person in her life, and this woman she had just now started to love.

Rue dried her tears quickly when they parted and she looked at Sax with serious eyes. "You may have a very long road ahead of you if you're trying to let go of Jenner. You should not have to let go. Keep her close. Keep her memory alive. You need to do that for yourself and for her daughter. Eventually, you may heal but the worst part will be learning to recover the part of you that went with Jenner."

"I agree," Sax said, nodding her head multiple times. She felt unbelievably connected to Rue right now. "Sometimes I don't know how to be me without her. And what Sax was really feeling, but she never said it, was she had not learned how to recover the part of her that left with Seth Moss either. And, now, having him just show up again had thrown her, what felt like, a thousand steps backward.

* * *

Zimmer walked out of the hospital feeling a little like he had just gotten out of prison. He was slow to move and not feeling like he wanted to do much more than make it to Seth's vehicle and be driven to the hotel, where he could just crawl into a bed again.

After Seth watched Zimmer fall fast asleep in one of the queen-sized beds in their hotel room, he left. He wanted to see Sax again.

As expected, Seth found the door to the lab locked. It was the only the entrance to the waiting area for patients who received blood withdrawal, but he couldn't get in. He checked the well-lit courtyard, but it was empty. He then decided to go into the cafeteria, order a cup of coffee, and just wait.

An hour and thirty minutes passed, and he was still waiting around. The cafeteria was busy at times, so he just passed the minutes by people watching. He was looking down at his empty coffee cup and had not seen her come in. She made it all the way to the check-out register with her cup of coffee and a banana in her hands. That's when Seth raised his head again and saw her from behind. The fitted denim on her lower body gave away her every curve. And those boots nearly up to her knees were sexy. Her hair flip flopped a bit on her head as she moved while she spoke. The way she brushed it away from covering her eye caught Seth's attention. *She was beautiful.*

He got up abruptly from his seat, leaving his empty coffee cup on the table, and he met her at the door before she exited the cafeteria. "How about sharing a cup with me?" he asked her, and she was startled.

"You scared the shit of me," she admitted, noticing she had moved too quickly and some of her coffee spilled over the side of the cup and dripped onto the white floor at her feet.

"Oh, sorry," he said, making a regretful face. "Join me?" he asked again.

"I'm working," she reminded him, and wanted to just start walking away, but her feet never moved.

"I'll take no more of your time than what you planned to break for…" he attempted to negotiate with her.

"Fine," she said, turning around and walking back into the cafeteria. He followed her inside and to a table. He sat down when she did and she frowned at him. "I thought we were doing coffee together?" He didn't have a cup in front of him, and he smiled that contagious smile of his. What she said had made him smile. *Together.* Doing anything together, with her, was something he never thought would again be possible for them.

"I don't want to waste my time getting in line now," he admitted and she left it at that. She could take as long of a break as she wanted, but she didn't tell him that. She would give him ten minutes, max.

"Are you going to eat that whole banana?" he asked her, seriously, and she rolled her eyes at him.

"I bought it, didn't I?" she asked, sarcastically.

"Yes, but…" he paused, "if I remember correctly, you could never finish a whole one. They make you gag."

Sax giggled. She couldn't help herself. He was right. She never could finish a *whole fucking banana,* as she sometimes referred to it. But, right now, out of spite, she wanted to eat the entire thing in front of him.

"I'm right, aren't I?" Seth smiled, feeling victorious. He remembered that small detail about her. And he had made her laugh.

"Are you going to waste your time talking about fruit?" she asked him, taking her first sip of coffee.

"Right, no," he replied. There was so much he wanted to say to her, but where to start was the problem. If he'd ask for her phone number, he knew she would balk because if she was in a relationship that would just be inappropriate. That's what he wanted to know first. "So, how long have you been in a relationship?" he asked her, and she looked up from her coffee cup, feeling speechless.

"I've had a few relationships since us," she began, already knowing she was embellishing. She had never had a relationship with any man since he left her. Only sex. "My current relationship means everything to me. This person in my life is my world. I don't know what I would do if anything ever happened to what we share." Seth knew he deserved this feeling now in the pit of his stomach and working its way up to his throat. But, still, he hated it. Hated knowing Sax had moved on, and felt so serious about someone else. Sax was well aware of what she was doing to him. She could see it in his eyes. The hurt she still carried made her want to make that bastard suffer. But, she didn't, and she added, "I love her so much."

"Her?" Seth asked, and his cheeks flushed. "You have a girlfriend now?" He could hardly choke out the words. *There was no way in hell she was gay.* He would have known. *Wouldn't he?*

"I'm referring to Quinn," she giggled, and Seth exhaled a loud sigh of relief.

"Holy Christ, Arynn!" he exclaimed, feeling amused and so incredibly relieved. *There was no man in Sax's life.* And Sax sat there, just taking in how he had called her Arynn. It had been a long time since she was called that.

"I spoke the truth. The love of my life right now is my best friend's daughter. She needs me, and I know I need her, too." Sax had suffered so much loss, and Seth felt terrible for her.

"So, in time, you may open yourself up to the idea of dating?" he asked her. "I mean, when you are settled into life with Quinn." Sax only wished she and Quinn could get settled into a life together. Zane stood in the way of that, and she feared he would for a long time.

Sax looked at the clock on the cafeteria wall. "Speaking of time, I need to get back to the lab," she told him. She didn't want to discuss dating.

"Answer my question first," he said, adding, "please." Gosh he wanted more time with her. What a fool he had been. The regret was killing him now more than ever once he had seen her and talked to her again.

"I don't want to date you," she said, adamantly, knowing exactly where he was going with his question. "I've been there, done that. We passed the point of dating each other when we lived together for three years. I gave you all of me. You were my world." Sax was thinking of what Rue had just said to her earlier. "The hardest part of losing you was trying over and over again to recover the part of me that went with you." *Damn, that made perfect sense.* "I don't know how much of me I've actually recovered from what you did to me, to us, but I do know that if I ever risked what I have left of myself, just to be with you again, it would be too much of a gamble." Sax stood up from where she was seated at the table with him, and she picked up her empty coffee cup. Before she walked away, she handed him the banana. "Here, you eat this. Bananas make me gag."

At that moment, Seth knew he would return to Chicago. He had to bring Zimmer back home. He belonged there. Seth, on the other hand, did not. He knew that for certain now. For Seth, this was not goodbye to Salem. Nor, to Sax.

Chapter 17

Zane Ski was in the basement of the old mansion, in his art studio. He was putting the finishing touches on that painting of the woman with a chic, short, cropped hairdo. The strands of hair nearly covering all of her right eye were exaggerated in the painting. Thicker, fuller, and somewhat eccentric. It was the first thing Zane wanted his eyes to move to. And while he didn't know if he would share this particular work of art with the world, he wanted that same reaction from everyone who laid eyes on it, if and when he did release it. The painting on his massive easel had crashed faced-down onto the concrete floor the night that crazed kid tried to gun down Zane and it had been ruined. Zane repainted Sax's image on a smaller scale this time. The easel was half the size and instead of creating an image that depicted her entire body, he chose to focus on her face and her neckline. The days and nights had run together for Zane as he was completely caught up in what he was painting, and feeling. If he didn't feel it, he couldn't paint it. That's just who he was.

It was ten-thirty-five at night and the basement, as Zane preferred when he painted, was quiet. He could hear the music coming from upstairs in Quinn's bedroom again, but it wasn't a distraction for him. He actually had gotten used to it, and liked it. Just as he liked having her there. They weren't close, but one day he knew they would be. His daughter gave him a reason to want to be a better man. He had finally found success as an artist and he wanted to continue to strive to be better. For her. He wanted to be worthy of Quinn's love, trust, and respect. He never measured up to her mother. Or, any woman. His infatuation with Jenner died with her. Now, he had moved on to her best friend. She was more his type anyway, he believed. Sax was a little rougher around the edges than the straight and narrow Jenner Wibbs.

Zane took three steps back and admired his work. One day, he thought, I will reveal this to Sax. And, maybe, just maybe, she will have the same reaction to it as she had when she fell for the painting upstairs of Jenner and the man slouching against that old barn with pain in his eyes as she walked away from him. That painting had a powerful effect on both of them. Zane never made love to a woman if he had not connected with her over art, first. Sax's reaction to his art, and to him, forced Zane into a freefall for her.

He stood there with a fire in his eyes, and then picked up his paintbrush again off the base of the easel. It wasn't quite there. It needed something more. Maybe more green in her eyes or more strokes of ash brown paint in the hair covering her right eye. Zane went back to work.

The old mansion was dark from the outside, with the exception of only a dim light coming from one window upstairs. The porch lights were off and the steps leading up to it were hard to see clearly in the pitch black of night. Zimmer placed one black cowboy boot on the bottom step, and so on, until he reached the front door. This time it didn't take any wavering. He tried the handle, turning it twice, but it was locked. He expected as much, knowing he truly had scared Zane Ski the last time. He may have acted like Zimmer was too young, clueless, and stupid. But, Zimmer knew better. He had the upper hand. If only everything had not gone wrong and he could have shot and killed him. *He deserved to die.*

Zimmer had not been able to put that out of his mind. He came to Salem to kill that man, and now Seth Moss was planning to drive them back to Chicago in the morning. His hospital stay and the wound that still burdened him with pain, deterred him some, but it didn't stop him.

When Seth had fallen asleep on the opposite queen-sized bed, Zimmer made his way out of his bed, got dressed, and left the room. He walked to the Wal-Mart Supercenter on West Main Street, which was open all night long. He purchased a portable gasoline tank there, and carried it right out of the store and through the streets of Salem to the nearest gas station. He already had matches in his pocket. He brought those along from the hotel room. He commended himself for thinking ahead. It would have looked suspicious buying both matches and a portable gasoline tank at the same time.

Zimmer bent down, below the porch steps, in the dark, and twisted off the cap on the gas tank. He then picked it up with his good arm, because his shoulder was feeling pained since he left the hotel. His pain medicine had worn off. It was more intense now and he knew he needed to pop a pill when he returned to the hotel. He was thinking in regards to an hour from now, and then he thought about tomorrow's trip back home. He wasn't at all ill at ease about what he was doing. His intention was to take a life inside of that house, and anyone who unfortunately was associated with that thief inside his home tonight.

He poured gasoline back and forth onto the three porch steps. Then he walked around to the right side of the house. He started pouring on the ground, close to the bottom row of siding on the house. There was some grass growing there, he could tell, even in the dark as he stepped, but mostly just dirt. There was no landscape around the old house. No rocks, pavers, bushes or anything to concern Zimmer about where to step. It was just flat ground. The perimeter of the house was bigger than Zimmer expected and he ran out of gasoline in the portable tank before he had made it the entire way around the house. He stopped about halfway on his path, on the left side of the house. *Good enough*, he thought as he dropped the empty tank where he was standing and walked back around to the front of the house. He stood near the steps of the front porch. The potent scent of gasoline was making him feel lightheaded. He knew he had splashed some onto his jeans and boots. Zimmer reached into the pocket of his black trench coat and retrieved a book of matches. He lit one and held it close to his face. He inhaled. He always did love that smell. Just as much as he loved playing with fire.

Zimmer let the first match burn entirely down, until it burned his fingers a little bit. With that burnt-out match still in his hand, he lit a second match and this time he was ready to throw it onto the porch steps. He knew the dangers of gasoline. It was extremely volatile, fumes would spread instantly and crazily over a large area in a short amount of time. And those fumes were highly explosive. He was aware of the serious harm it could bring and how it destroyed everything in its path.

He ran backwards, fast, probably too fast, because he had jerked his body and pain that made him wince instantly radiated through his chest and shoulder. He lit another match as he ran around to the right side of the house. And another in the back. The flames, by now, had lit up the entire yard and were spreading fiercely. One more match on the opposite side of the house and Zimmer knew he had to get out of there. The final match was lit as he ran and threw it onto the ground, close to the side of the house that had not yet gone up in flames. His foot came down on something in the grass, tripped him, and he fell forward. The in-ground entrance to the cellar was just a few feet away, and Zimmer ended up falling head first into it. He landed hard inside that cramped space and his body hurt everywhere. He looked up with sheer panic in his eyes as the flames had already surrounded the ground above the cellar.

There was no escape. His screams went unheard. That old mansion, vacant for years, sat on a dead-end street with no other homes or businesses nearby for decades. Zimmer had been careless when he dropped the gas tank in the grass and just left it there, unbeknownst to him that he would trip over it minutes later. And that would cost him his life.

Chapter 18

Seth woke up and immediately noticed the bed beside his in the room was empty. He got up to check the bathroom, but the door to it was open and the room was dark. He turned on the lights now and noticed Zimmer's boots and coat were gone. Seth hurried to slip into his jeans and the Chicago Bears hoodie he had worn earlier. He wasn't going to ignore how strange this seemed, and he was worried.

When he walked through the hotel's lobby, he caught the eye of the front desk clerk. The young male said *hello* first. It was nearly midnight and not unusual for guests to check out at all hours. "Hi," Seth spoke in return. "Have you, by chance, seen a young, Taiwanese man come through here tonight?"

"No, I have not," the clerk responded.

"Okay, thanks anyway," Seth said as he just stood there for a moment, wondering where he would begin to look for Zimmer now. He was hoping he had just taken a walk down to the lobby for a soda or something. Seth had his car keys in his front jeans pocket, so he thought to take a drive through the streets of Salem. He knew Zimmer was in no condition to take a long walk, but maybe he hadn't gone far to get some fresh air.

Seth had his hand on the glass door, ready to push it open when he heard sirens in the distance and the sound forced the desk clerk to run to the large window near his computer. "That's the second time now. Those are Odin fire trucks, a neighboring town. I guess they've been called for backup." Seth already knew that detail. He had grown up here.

"Where's the fire?" Seth asked him.

"At the old mansion on the east edge of town!" the desk clerk seemed excited to report that to Seth, and Seth's eyes widened. He felt panicked. And he just knew. Zimmer had gone out. They were leaving town tomorrow and he had not gotten his revenge. Seth was afraid of what really had been going through Zimmer's mind. He had heard some of the ER nurses gossiping about him at the hospital. One of them said they heard the police were suspicious of *him*, and not the artist who lived in the old mansion. Zane had brushed off what he overheard. He knew Zimmer. He was an innocent kid who had been messed with and he was angry. But, now, Seth wondered just how deep his anger was rooted.

Seth ran out of the hotel and got into his Explorer. He turned the key quickly into the ignition and drove out of the parking lot. His destination was the east edge of town.

She stopped at a four-way stop and her eyes widened when three fire trucks, one following on the tail of the other, were to the right of her. Sax had just completed her work with Rue in the hospital lab, and she was driving home. She was tired and her thoughts were sporadic as she drove through the dark streets. But, when she saw and heard those fire trucks coming, she had a rush of those familiar pangs of panic. She was not home when her parents' house burned to the ground with them still inside. It had been twelve years and she still ached from that horrendous loss. Her mother. Her father. Her home. Her belongings. All had gone up in flames. Sax never saw those flames. By the time she was brought back from her camping trip by the parents of her friends, there was nothing but ruins left. Black, charred. Everything was gone.

Sax froze at that four-way stop, and when the last fire truck sped through, she watched all three of them consecutively turn down a dead-end street. No one lived down there, there wasn't single business down there. That was the route to Zane's old mansion. Sax lifted her right foot off of the brake pedal and pressed down hard on the gas. She had to be sure. She told herself it wasn't. It couldn't be. But, still, she would drive down there.

Sax could see the fire trucks, there were at least six of them, lining that dead-end street. She knew where they were headed as soon as she met those emergency trucks in a rush at the four-way stop. She parked her car mid-block, and got out of it to run. As she reached the house, Seth was behind the wheel of his Explorer and also turning onto that dead-end street.

Sax ran hard and fast and the feelings of panic were overwhelming her. She reached the curb in front of Zane's house, a place she had parked so many times. She saw his old, rundown Mustang. And now, a few firefighters as well as policemen, standing outside in the yard near the rickety wooden fence, noticed her. They watched her face, they saw her look at the house, fully engulfed in flames. She started eye level and ended up moving her head further up to where the rooftop would be, but was no more. There were high, bright orange flames in its place. She felt the weight of the world come crashing down on her at that moment. She started to move her feet, and a sprint quickly became a frantic run. She was stopped by three firefighters as soon as she reached the front yard. She was repeatedly screaming *No* and a name that they all could clearly make out as *Quinn*. Then, they watched her turn away and heard a scream directed at the heavens, begging in desperation, *Jenner, please do something!*

She cried and she screamed and then fell to her knees as a strong voice came from one of the firefighters, insisting how she had to stay back. She cried out, asking if anyone had made it out of the house, *a twelve-year-old girl with long, blonde hair, a tall, thin man with a ponytail,* and the firefighter's reply broke what was left of her already bruised and battered heart.

As Seth made his way, running down the middle of that dead-end street, he saw what he feared earlier. The flames, the smoke, how emergent it was for the firefighters to act fast to extinguish a massive fire to save lives and property. This could not have been the act of his new friend, a young man who he was just getting to know. But, really, Seth had barely known him. Seth felt like a fool. *A fucking fool.* Had Zimmer really done this? *Was the kid, who he had just spent the past three days and nights with, capable of murder?*

Seth made his way in between the fire trucks and through the open gate on the wooden fence. He saw a few firefighters in a huddle, so he ran up to them. And then he noticed a distraught woman in the mix. He saw immediately it was Sax, but he could not register why she was there.

"Sax!" he raised his voice and caught her attention as well as the firefighters with her. Sax looked over at him, but never moved. She, too, wondered why he was there but her thought process was so unclear right now that she didn't even care to know. She felt as she had when she found out her parents were gone. And again when she heard that Jenner was dead. This pain, the pain of knowing Quinn had burned up in that house, was the last straw for Sax. She was done. This life, her life, meant nothing to her anymore. How one person was expected to get up and dust herself off after everything she had gone through in her thirty years was now beyond her. She no longer wanted to carry the pain, accept the burdens, or even attempt to move on. If there were no firemen, and now Seth, standing there with her, she may have just walked into that burning house and never looked back. She wanted to join her parents, Jenner, and now sweet Quinn, on the other side. This side, by herself, was suffocating her. The pain had reached the endpoint for her. It was just too much to bear.

Seth moved closer and grabbed Sax by both of her shoulders. It was the first time he had touched her in years, and she felt nothing. She was numb and he sensed how lost she was. "Tell me what's going on!" he demanded. "What is your connection to this home? I heard an artist lived here," he added, wondering if Zimmer had been there, started that horrendous fire, and made his way back to the hotel by now.

Seth led her over to the fence as he heard one of the fireman yell out a reminder for them to *continue to stay back!* "Sax, talk to me! You're scaring me!" Seth tried again to get her to speak.

"I, I lost, her." That was all Sax said before pausing. "Quinn, my girl, was in that house." Seth felt the blood drain from his face. *The girl he had just met at Sax's house. The girl who had just lost her mother. The one person Sax had described as being her whole world.*

"Oh my God!" he spoke, feeling scared and helpless and not wanting to believe that Zimmer could be responsible for killing both the artist and that girl. "That girl? Why was she in there?" Seth felt sick to his stomach.

"She was his daughter. Her birth father lived there." Sax replied, almost in a whisper, but Seth had heard her every word. And he was feeling her pain, too. This woman had been through too much. Being at the scene of this fire alone, he knew, was a brutal reminder of what she lost as a teenager. She used to confide in him, with tears and anger, about what it felt like to lose her parents the night she graduated from high school. A time in her life when she was supposed to feel as if the world was at her fingertips as her whole life was ahead of her and endless dreams and goals were possible. Instead, she felt as if her world had slipped through her finger tips and she into a trench that would always be too deep to climb out of. Alone.

Seth didn't know what to say, so he chose to do what felt right. He pulled her close and held her as tight as he possibly could. She sunk into his grip and fell apart.

When the sun came up from behind the clouds, Sax could have cursed the symbolism that it was a new day. The world continued on, once again, when she suffered a loss. She was sitting on the cold ground, with her back up against that old wooden fence. The firefighters were still there, and so was Seth. He never left her side. He spoke when she wanted to, and otherwise he just held her, or sat close in case she needed him.

Sax had told him repeatedly that she was not leaving there until the bodies were found. She had to know. Seth agreed, and he continuously had thoughts of Zimmer racing through his mind. He had sent him multiple texts, but he hadn't responded.

The ruins were ground-level now. That historical building, erected in 1852, was no more. It was part of Salem's history. Sax didn't care about any of that though. All she cared about was the mere fact that one person who did not make it out of that house alive was supposed to be her future. She had presently been living every day for her, since she lost Jenner. Together, they were making it. They were powering through the pain and grief because they had each other. *Now, what?* Sax thought to herself. And nothing came to mind.

One firefighter was circling the grounds. Seth watched him and wondered what type of protocol he was following. The air was thick with black smoke as daylight emerged, and Sax was quiet on the ground beside Seth when they and everyone else within earshot heard the scream of that lone firefighter who had been circling the house on foot.

Seth pulled Sax up to her feet and they ran around to the left side of the house, alongside of the firemen and police officers who were on the scene. *A body. In the cellar. A gas can in the grass.* Both Seth and Sax took it all in, but it was only Seth who understood. And he was the only one who wasn't surprised when a body was brought up. Being on lower ground beneath the flames had kept the body from being completely burned and unrecognizable. Seth knew it was Zimmer.

He never said a word, but he knew he had to. Seth needed to pull aside a police officer on those very grounds. He knew what happened. He had the answers for them, or at least he thought he did. Seth was consumed with regret for having been the person who brought Zimmer to Salem. He was indirectly responsible for the death of two people. And one of them was a little girl who meant the world to Sax. He couldn't face her with that truth. She would find out, but he would already be gone, on his way back to Chicago by then. He didn't want to see the look in her eyes when she would blame him. He wasn't man enough to handle her hating him. He had hurt her terribly once before, but since he arrived back in Salem he had sensed that she could forgive him. He had wanted so badly to make it all up to her. But, now he knew that dream had perished tonight along with those three people on the east edge of Salem.

Seth was staring at Zimmer's body and was lost in his own hopeless thoughts when Sax touched his arm. "You okay?"

"Not really," he said. "This is all just so sickening." Before Sax could agree with him, the fire chief approached them both.

"It's time for you both to go," he said, knowing what they had been waiting around for. "We pulled one body from the house, the basement. A male was found on the stairwell, clinging to a painting in his arms.

Oh my, Zane, Sax silently strung those words together in her mind. "Wait!" she spoke. "Upstairs? Was there… a… girl?" she choked on her words as the tears trickled off her face and Seth put his arm tightly around her shoulders.

"No," the fire chief responded. He didn't want to say that she could have been so badly burned, nothing was left of her body but ashes. He couldn't say that to this woman. It was killing him enough thinking about his own little girl at home, the same age as he had heard the girl was inside of this house.

Sax wanted to have hope, but no one was giving it or encouraging it. So, she knew not to. She just cried harder as Seth pulled her into his thick, broad chest and she allowed him to.

Chapter 19

Sax said she could drive home by herself. Seth offered to be there for her, drive her, but she insisted on being alone. She was so withdrawn and any comfort she had accepted from him through the night and early morning hours was now over. She wanted to go home, alone, and Seth knew he had to respect that. It was time for him to visit the Salem Police Department now to fill in the blanks for them.

She pulled her car into the garage and immediately closed the garage door, wanting to shut out the world again. She smelled so badly of smoke from being terribly close to the burning house all night long. Her face, neck and hands, the only flesh visible in the cold air, felt as if there was a film on it. If she looked in the mirror, Sax would see the soot visible on her face. She had seen it on Seth, beside her for hours on end.

She made her way into the kitchen and threw her keys onto the high vintage table with sea green stools. She was going to move through the living room and straight down the hallway to the bathroom. If only she could step into the shower and wash away the pain and grief that came into her life again.

As she stepped, one foot in front of the other, her favorite white afghan caught her eye on the sofa. And then she experienced a feeling she would never forget for as long as she lived. Under that afghan, all covered up on her pale yellow sofa was Quinn, sound asleep.

"Oh my God, you're alive!" Sax exclaimed with laughter and tears at the same time. She instantly startled Quinn awake. She had just forced open her eyes and Sax had thrown herself beside her, hugging her neck and kissing her face. Her tears were spilling over onto Quinn's cheeks.

Quinn kept hearing Sax repeatedly say, *you're alive,* and she was confused. "Sax, stop. You're scaring me. Did something happen?"

Sax pulled herself together. Her heart felt such relief and was bursting with joy. "Were you here all night?" Sax asked, with a wide smile plastered on her face.

"Yes, I turned on the music in my room like I always do and I left. I knew you were working so I let myself in with my key and waited for you. I planned to go home late, but you never came and I must have fallen asleep. How mad is my dad?" Quinn really didn't care. She was more upset at the idea that her cover was blown. She would never be successful at sneaking out of the house again.

"You are so smart and I love you so much! I know your mom was with you and guiding you away from the danger last night," Sax spoke. "I have to tell you something, sweetie. And, it's bad, very bad, but you are here, you are okay, and I'm never letting you leave me again." Quinn's eyes were wide as she listened. "There was a fire at the old mansion last night," Sax could not bring herself to say *your house*. It was Zane's off the wall idea to live there, and anywhere with him for that matter had not felt right to Quinn, nor to Sax. "Someone set fire to it, and that person died on the grounds last night. I thought you were inside, I thought it was too late, I thought you were-"

"I'm okay, Sax..." Quinn said, trying to stop the tears that were freely flowing again on the face of a woman she trusted and loved so much. "But, my dad isn't, is he? He's dead, isn't he?" Quinn imagined he had been in the basement, in his studio, in full artist mode, and had not even known the house was on fire until it was too late.

Sax nodded her head and pulled this little girl into her arms. This little girl who had grown up so much since she met her six years ago, and especially in the past few months since her mother had died. They both cried, but neither of them were consumed with sadness. This was a tragedy that had, in turn, given them a renewed hope for the present and especially their future. Together.

Seth left the police station after being there for two and a half hours. He told the captain, who remembered him from the scene of the fire, everything he knew. He filled in blanks that inevitably made perfect sense to the police. Because there was an intruder and a shooting at the mansion just two nights prior, the police had pinned the house fire on Jason Zimmer hours before they discovered his body right there on the steps leading to the cellar. The story added up. The police were grateful to Seth and he was assured that he was free to go.

Seth hardly felt free though. He felt to blame for that man and child's death. He felt used by a young kid who he had trusted, liked, and enjoyed taking under his wing. But, Jason Zimmer was a phony. He was a crazed maniac who had plotted murder. He was actually the one who had pulled a gun on that artist first. He had lied to Seth about everything.

Seth went back to the hotel to gather his things. He stepped over and ignored all of Zimmer's possessions. And left it behind for the hotel or the police to deal with. He wanted no part of any of it.

Seth thought of Sax as he drove out of town. When he arrived back in Salem, he wasn't sure what he would find if he looked her up. Her life wasn't at all as he expected. She had not moved on, she had not been able to let go of what they shared. She had endured too much pain, because of him, and then because her best friend died. Seth had felt so close to seizing a chance to reuniting with her. She needed him as much as he needed her. They weren't complete without each other. He loved how much she wanted to share her life with the little girl

159

her best friend had left behind. And, then, he was partly responsible for taking her away from Sax. Had he not come to town at Zimmer's urging, that little girl would be alive still. And Sax wouldn't be broken. As he drove, he cried.

Sax gave in and told Quinn she could go to school. She let her borrow some athletic clothes from her closet, which were only a little bit baggy, and she promised to take her shopping after school as her entire wardrobe was lost in the fire. There was only one thing Quinn had to do for Sax now. And she agreed. She accompanied her to the Salem Police Department. The entire force was overjoyed to know that child had not lost her life in the fire.

Sax was asked to speak with the captain alone while Quinn ate donuts for breakfast with a police officer who she knew as the mother of one of her classmates.

Sax was stunned to learn of Seth's involvement with Zimmer. She knew he was in town with a friend, and she knew there was an accident. She had never found out that Zane was involved and shot the man who was hospitalized. The captain pieced all of it together for her, and he informed her of Seth's part in aiding them to close the case without unanswered questions.

The captain shared with Sax how distraught Seth was, believing a child's life was lost. Sax knew he must have been afraid to tell her the truth. She was both angry and touched by that, which made no sense to her. Seth cared about her, Sax knew that. But, what he did, trusting a stranger and escorting him into town, could have ended as Sax believed it had all night long. Quinn could have died, and he was right to assume she never would have forgiven him for that.

✳ ✳ ✳

Sax dropped off Quinn at school and reminded her of what they were going to do right after school. "I know, I know, shop until we drop!" Quinn said, humoring Sax, because Sax was the one who loved to go shopping. Not Quinn. Quinn preferred to order what she wanted online. "Yes, you are partly correct," Sax had told her. "But, we, as in you and I, are also going to kick off the rest of our lives together." Quinn smiled back at her before she got out of the car and what she said had melted Sax's heart. "You're the next best thing to my mom."

Sax was still thinking about that comment, which she considered to be the utmost praise coming from the daughter of her best friend. She shifted her car into park, got out, and walked through the brown, winter-weather-beaten grass, and up to the gravestone which had etched on it the name Jenner Wibbs. She just stood there for a long while, silent. She had not been there, to that dreadful cemetery, since the day they put her best friend in the ground.

"You don't belong here," Sax finally spoke. "I know shit happens and sometimes lives end before they are supposed to. I know that all too well, remember? I'm the woman who has an eighteen-year-old girl trapped inside of this shell as I feel like that was the day my life froze. My parents were lost to me, then it wasn't by death but Seth was lost to me, too. You came along and saved me in so many ways, but the night you left me I retracted to those old feelings of being helpless and hopeless." Sax sighed and wiped away a few tears that had trickled down both of her cheeks. "Last night, I thought I lost Quinn. God, that pain. I know it was you. I know you got her ass out of that house. Thank you. You not only saved her, but you saved me. God, I love you and miss you and wish you were here." More tears flooded her eyes and freefell down her cheeks as she spoke. "I know you're not in this fucking hard, cold ground." Sax beat the block heel of her boot onto the ground. "I know you're with us. Alive in our hearts. It's not easy, but we are making it."

Sax kept pausing and thinking before she spoke. This was the last thing she wanted to say to Jenner, right here, right now. "I need to know what I am supposed to do," Sax began. "You know he came back. You know I still love him and need him in so many ways. He has regrets. I know he wants a do-over. I don't know if I can. I told him I won't, but I think he could see right through me. You know I'm not as tough as I come across. Seth has always known that, too. Jenner, guide me, please."

Sax left the cemetery in tears. *How fucking unfair was it for her to have to leave her best friend there?* Sax, understandably, hated cemeteries. She had not gone to visit her parent's graves more than a few times and always left swearing she would never be back. She felt the same way today, leaving Jenner.

In addition, having no sign from Jenner upset her, too. Sax hadn't sensed her in awhile. She was incredibly grateful for the protection Quinn received last night. And, now, she felt selfish, but she wanted a sign. She wanted to know. She wanted to be at peace about letting go of Seth Moss.

Chapter 20

Sax watched a man with jet black hair, combed neatly on his head, sit down and roll up the sleeve on his left arm. He was wearing a green and blue plaid shirt. He wasn't a tall or big man. In fact, before he sat down, Sax noticed he was even in height with her, and she was wearing ballet flats again.

She looked at his chart before she began the blood withdrawal. "Have you fasted since midnight?" she asked, noticing he was only having a cholesterol check completed.

"Yes," he answered, nodding. Sax then asked him for his date of birth and when he told her, she calculated that he was forty years old.

The needle went smoothly into his vein, and Sax noticed him looking away. He was staring at the opposite wall. In her profession, she was aware of how many people could not handle a simple blood draw. Needles were a fear. The sight of blood was sickening for some. "You okay?" Sax asked him, forcing him to look away from the wall and up at her, standing over his arm.

"Mmm hmm," he answered, and Sax noticed his pale face.

"Almost done," she added, and quickly pulled out the needle and placed a piece of cotton on the bend of his arm, applying pressure.

"I'm a wus with this," the man said to Sax, after she turned around from placing the vial of blood in a container to hold it upright on the sterile counter top.

Sax smiled at him, "No worries. Most people are." She noticed he still looked pale. "Do you need to keep sitting there for a few minutes? I can get you an orange juice or something?"

"Oh, I'm fine," he responded, beginning to stand up, slowly. "You're making a fuss just like my mother does when I come here."

Sax didn't respond for a moment, as she stared at him, and thought the only person working in that lab who was old enough to be the mother of a forty-year-old man was Rue. "Are you Rue's son?" she asked as soon as the thought popped into her mind.

"That I am," he replied. "I'm Liam Bray."

Sax thought how she should have made that connection when she read his name on the chart, but she had not really paid much attention at the time. "Well, small world," Sax said to him. "I'm Sax Arynn."

"Nice to meet you, Sax," Liam said, not offering his hand and appearing a little bit timid, or maybe just more reserved than anything.

"You too," she replied. "I know Rue has three children, and four grandchildren. What number are you?" Sax immediately wondered if he was Rue's oldest. The baby who was fathered by a man she had an affair with.

"I'm number one, her firstborn son," Liam said, standing not too far from Sax and again she noticed he was short, for a man. She was five-seven so she knew he was as well. "I have a brother and a sister, those two are responsible for giving our mother her grandchildren."

"No children for you?" Sax asked, not wanting to pry. She assumed all of Rue's children were married.

"My ex-wife had the final say-so with that," Liam said, looking somewhat disappointed.

"I see," Sax replied, not knowing what else to say. She really didn't want his life story and suddenly they were saved by Rue sticking her upper body around the curtain.

"I thought that was your voice!" she said, smiling at Liam as if he was still her little boy, and Sax grinned.

"Hello mom," Liam said, acting as if he was going to exit the room now.

"Very nice to meet your boy," Sax said to Rue and she laughed a little. Sax noticed she looked pale now, too. She wished it was something in that room, or a virus traveling around, but for Rue she knew that was not the case. Sax then wondered if Rue had told her children that her leukemia had come back. And, that she was refusing treatment.

"He is my handsome one," she giggled, "but don't tell your brother I said so!" Rue laughed out loud and Sax immediately picked up on how partial she was to her firstborn son, the product of an affair with the one lover she had never gotten over.

Liam looked over at Sax and smiled. He held her eyes for a moment. She was going to tell him to have a good day, or wait for his mother to do the same, but he spoke first as he moved the curtain away from his mother and made room for himself to exit through the doorway. "I'm not usually this forward," he began, looking at Sax's face after he had taken note how she was not wearing a wedding ring on her left hand, "and how embarrassing to ask this in front of my mother, but would you be interested in having a drink with me this evening?"

Sax's eyes widened. He was a handsome man, a little on the short-side, but built well. No beer gut, yet, at age forty. He had just asked her out on a date, and in front of Rue. *And he was related to Rue.* "I'm flattered," she replied, brushing the hair away from her right eye as a nervous reaction right now, "but, I can't. I just received custody of a twelve year old and I need to focus on her for awhile."

Liam nodded his head and replied, "I understand." He told his mother goodbye and then looked back at Sax. "If you were to change your mind, you can always find me at The Wine Rack." Sax was familiar with that little wine shop on Main Street and their back room bar as a popular hangout. She and Seth had gone there together many times. The idea of meeting Liam there didn't appeal to her. She didn't need another reminder of Seth.

She had not seen or heard from him since they parted ways in front of the charred ruins of the old mansion. She assumed he had returned to Chicago again, because that's where he wanted to be. She spent a few days feeling disappointed in him again. Then she told herself to focus on her life with Quinn, which was just beginning.

When Liam left, Rue stepped into the small room and closed the curtain. When Sax looked over at her, she was shaking her head. "What?" Sax asked.

"My son has been divorced for ten months, and he has not been ready for another woman. Has not been on one single date. He comes in here for a blood draw and takes one look at you and he's smitten." Sax grinned a little. She felt flattered, but that was all. "I never would have pegged you for his type," Rue began again. "You would have to quit that damn smoking, that's for sure!"

Sax was now annoyed, but what else was new when it came to Rue? "He told me he's your firstborn," Sax said to Rue, on purpose, to take a jab at her.

"Hey, now, behave yourself," Rue said, looking serious. "He can never know!"

"Relax," Sax responded. "Your son and I will probably never see each other again."

When she arrived home from work, Sax walked through the kitchen door from the garage and found Quinn perched up on one of the kitchen chairs. "Well, hello there," Sax said to her, loving this feeling of having her living there, all of the time now. Sax had immediately gone to her lawyer to have the papers drawn up to officially adopt Quinn. She wanted legal custody of her, just in case there would be another man out there somewhere claiming to be Quinn's father one day. Sax smiled to herself. Jenner would put her in a painful headlock for thinking that, but that's why Sax momentarily amused herself with that thought. Jenner never slept around. That was why her one-night-stand with Zane Ski was so shocking. "So what's our plan for tonight?" Sax asked, excited for it to be Friday night and she was not scheduled to work at all this weekend.

"Well," Quinn replied, "I guess whatever you want to do."

"What does that mean? Is there something fun going on?" Sax meant fun for them, but Quinn's reply didn't quite match hers.

"Emily and Lauren are having a sleepover..." Quinn was careful to mention, "and they want me to come."

Sax replied, "Oh, okay," and then she realized again how this child was a preteen and she would want to put her friends first. Sometimes. And, maybe, even all of the time, for many years ahead. Once again, Sax could have cursed Jenner for leaving them during these crucial years.

"What do you want to do?" Sax asked, nonchalantly. She didn't want it to be obvious to Quinn that she felt disappointed.

"I'd like to go..." Quinn said, "but I don't want to leave you hanging. I know you were excited to plan something together."

Sax smiled. "Quinnster, don't you worry about me. I want to see you happy and having a good time with your friends. I will be here tomorrow and every day after that for you!"

"I know you will, thank you," Quinn said, smiling, and Sax told her to go pack a bag for her sleepover.

It was seven o'clock when Sax walked back into her empty house. She was wearing her favorite gray sweatpants and black half-zip pullover. Her feet were bare as she walked into the living room and sat down on the end of the pale yellow sofa. Turning on the television didn't interest her, nor did reading a book. She thought about pouring herself a glass of wine instead of eating something for dinner. Then, she thought about The Wine Rack. She didn't get asked out all that much anymore. And now, raising Quinn, she knew her life was going to be different. She couldn't always just come and go for an impromptu night out. Or date. *If Liam Bray was having a drink at the back room bar, maybe she would join him afterall?*

The entrance to the bar was behind the store. Sax got out of her car and stood outside in her dark-washed flared denim, two-inch black stilettos, and a black wide-ribbed turtleneck sweater. There were only about a half a dozen cars in the parking lot, and no one was coming or going at the moment. Sax lit a cigarette before going inside. She thought of Rue and her comment about her son not approving. *Oh well,* Sax smirked as she inhaled that nicotine she so craved, *to each his own.*

A few minutes later, Sax opened the door, leading into the bar. She didn't recognize the faces she glanced at by the bar and she was glad she hadn't. It had been a long time since she stepped foot in there. It had been remodeled since and a new bartender was hired. *Out with the old, in with the new,* Sax thought, and then she spotted Liam. He had been sitting at the opposite end of the bar and was now walking toward her. He was wearing the same jeans she remembered from the hospital, but now a different plaid shirt. This one, had purple and red colors in it.

"Sax Arynn, you came anyway," Liam said, talking a little louder than he had in the hospital, as he was trying to be heard over the music in the bar. Sax still noticed how he was soft-spoken.

"I did," she replied, "Turns out my twelve year old has a more active social life than I do on a Friday night." Liam laughed out loud, and Sax was smiling because it had felt really nice to be able to say *my* twelve year old. She felt so at peace, and that could have been why she opted to show up there tonight. *Out with the old, in with the new?*

✳ ✳ ✳

Three glasses later of The Wine Rack's house wine, always a favorite of Sax's, and she was enjoying Liam's company more than she had expected.

"So you're in sales?" Sax asked him, gathering as much from what he had been talking about.

"Sort of," Liam replied. "I own Salem Hardware and Rental, on the corner of Delmar and Whittaker."

"Really? I know that store well. I used to go in there with my dad," Sax remembered those days so well. She had eighteen years of memories and every one, big or small, was so meaningful now.

"Well then your dad must have known my dad," Liam said, "because mine owned the store before I did. You probably know from working with my mom that nine years ago he died unexpectedly from a heart-attack. I was unhappy as a car salesman, and I had always wanted to be just like my dad. So, I took over his business." Sax smiled at him, thinking how wonderful that was, and she even commended Rue, to herself, for keeping a secret for all the right reasons.

"I lost my father, too," Sax offered, and Liam was a little surprised to hear that, considering she was at least ten years younger than him. "Our house caught fire the night of my high school graduation. I was out of town, camping with my friends for one last hurrah before we all separated for college. My parents both died that night."

"I'm so sorry. How unbelievable," Liam spoke, sitting across a private table from her and looking into her eyes. He could see the pain was still so very evident.

"Yeah, only it becomes very believable very quickly when you're eighteen and all alone. No grandparents, or other family. A lot of people want to help, initially, and then time goes on, people resume *their* lives, *their* normalcy, and I've spent the last twelve years still looking for mine." Sax thought she had found it when she met Seth, but she didn't say that right now. She didn't want to think about Seth Moss while she had a really nice man in front of her, and she was enjoying him.

"I can relate on some level," Liam said, reaching across the table to touch her hand, and she didn't mind. "My ex-wife and I were never *really* happy together. I didn't feel as if I had found where I was supposed to be, or who I was meant to be with. But, as a husband and a man who is loyal to those he loves, I gave it my all."

Sax was listening intently. This man seemed so genuine. There had to be more to him. It didn't really matter to her though if there was another shoe to drop. This was just one night, sharing drinks with someone who was pleasant to be around. "So, she's the one who wanted out of your marriage?" Sax asked, feeling comfortable enough to pry a little, and sinking into the effects of her third glass of wine.

"No," Liam responded. "I did. She got pregnant with another man's baby. I couldn't handle that. She said it was over and begged me to raise the baby as mine. I could not. One, she cheated on me. And, two, I could never overcome something like that."

Sax's eyes widened. "You mean being with someone who had cheated?" she asked, knowing what he was going to answer, and not believing the irony of life. Liam was not the biological son of the man who raised him.

172

"No," Liam shook his head, and took a long swig of his beer in the bottle in front of him. "I cannot wrap my head around the prospect of raising another man's child." Sax thought he seemed naïve or maybe she was just worldlier than he was. The idea of raising Quinn felt amazing to her. But, the circumstances were altogether different. No one cheated. Her best friend died.

Sax thought of Rue then. She was a smart woman. She had known her husband, born and raised in a small town and still living there, would never accept another man's son as his own. Rue did what she had to do. And, her story really did have a happy ending. At least it did for her husband and three children. Sax wondered if Rue wished as the years passed that she could have made a life with her lover. If only he had wanted her as badly as she wanted him. Sax knew that feeling all too well and what it felt like to live with it, for years.

That subject was dropped between them and after one more glass of wine, Sax said she needed to get going. Liam stood up first. "Me, too," he said. "I'll walk out with you." Sax had intended to have a cigarette outside, but she wouldn't in front of him. Rue's comment still stung a little. She would just smoke on the way home while she drove.

When they stepped outside, the night air was chilly, but not too cold. That instantly reminded her of Jenner and the night they left the Mexican restaurant, drunk. Their hug in the parking lot, between their cars, was their last.

"You okay?" Liam asked Sax as he watched her face as they walked together to her car. He wondered if she had too much to drink, maybe she had a low tolerance for alcohol, and he should offer to drive her.

"Yes, I'm good," she replied, pushing the sad thought of that life-changing night out of her mind. She had a good time tonight, with Liam, and she wanted to focus on that. "Thank you for the wine and conversation, it was nice." Sax spoke, making direct eye contact with him, and that was so easy to do because he was the same height. If he would not have been wearing those snakeskin brown cowboy boots, while she was wearing stilettos tonight, she may have towered him.

"You're very welcome, it was nice," Liam replied as Sax used her remote car keys to unlock her door. Before she opened it by the handle, she turned and rested her bottom up against the driver's side window. "We should do it again...sometime," Liam said, as he stepped closer and Sax suddenly knew she was trapped. It wasn't a bad thing. The feeling she was having right now was nice. It wasn't overwhelming or suffocating. Liam leaned in and met his lips with hers. It was sweet at first. Sort of like butter melting in her mouth, and on her tongue. Their kiss quickly escalated from sweet to intense. Her hands were around the back of his neck, her fingers in his jet-black hair, and he held her around the waist. She was in shape and he could feel her tight abs. He put more of his weight on her as her body was pressed up against the car window. He was a good kisser, but Sax could sense his desperation and desire. She remembered Rue telling her how Liam had not dated in the ten months since he had gotten divorced. She wondered if *not dating* meant he had not had sex. It sort of felt like that right now, and she pulled away before he dropped his pants and screwed her standing upright under the streetlight.

He stopped, but didn't move away. Their bodies remained pressed together and their hands were still on each other. "Do you want to follow me back to my place?" he asked her, and Sax immediately thought about the night one kiss with Zane led to immediate sex. She really was not that kind of a woman. She wondered now if Liam had truly enjoyed their time inside The Wine Rack tonight, or if he had just wanted to bed her.

"No," Sax responded, hoping he would back up and off of her so she could have some wiggle room to open her car door and get inside.

"Can I see you again?" Liam asked her.

"Maybe," Sax responded, not really feeling all that sure she wanted to.

"How about sharing your cell number with me?" he stated, moving toward her to kiss her open-mouthed again.

She stopped his kiss by responding lightly and then pulling away quickly. "How about, if I want to call you, I'll ask your mother for your number," she said, feeling sarcastic and Liam laughed, but he looked as if he wasn't amused. More like disappointed.

When Sax drove out of that parking lot, she wondered if she would ever again find a man who made her feel like Seth had. She missed him. She had never stopped missing him.

Chapter 21

When Sax walked into the lab on Monday morning, Rue gave her a warm smile. Sax returned a smile to her, and told herself not to read anything into the look. Surely, her son, a grown man, had not told his mother what happened between them. There really wasn't anything to tell. They had a few drinks, easy conversation, and then they made out a little in the parking lot until she felt like he was going to whip out his manhood and expect her to allow him to take care of business. The more Sax thought about it, the more unnerved she felt.

"So, word on the street is someone changed her mind about dating my son," Rue, as usual, was direct and Sax felt like puking in the trash can beside the door where she had just walked in.

"First of all, that's not the word on the street," Sax began, "it's straight from your boy's mouth. In addition, we are not dating. My plans changed Friday night, so I met him for a few drinks."

"He said you kissed him," Rue added, widening her eyes and looking ridiculous to Sax.

"I kissed him?" Sax asked, recalling Liam's tongue initiating so much of their kiss.

Rue giggled out loud. "Oh, I won't pry for any further details. Liam keeps me quite informed though." Rue winked, and Sax all but threw up in her mouth. *He was one of those sons. Too close for comfort to mommy.*

"He's a nice guy, Rue, but I have no room in my life right now for any man," Sax meant those words.

"Love, sometimes, comes along when we least expect it..." Rue stated, and it was Sax's turn to widen her eyes.

"Love?" she asked.

"I know my son," Rue replied. "Now, we just need to get you to kick that bad nicotine habit."

"I am not in love, nor will I be falling in love with your son," Sax stated, raising her voice. "And, you make me want a cigarette right now!"

Sax was done talking to Rue for the rest of the day. What she had said, about her son, and in reference to their date, had further turned off Sax.

She didn't know what made her do it, but she didn't rethink it either. Sax stopped by the Salem Police Department on her way home from work. She walked in through the double glass doors and made her way into the spacious lobby. Then, she asked the receptionist if she could speak to the captain.

He remembered her from the night of the fire, as he offered her a metal folding chair in front of his desk. The carpet was an old, ugly red, his desk was small and made of dark wood that was either rotting or chipping away in spots. "What can I do for you, Ms. Arynn?" he asked her as he too sat down behind his desk. His seat was nothing more than a folding chair as well.

"The night of the fire…you remember a man named Seth Moss there, right?" Sax asked.

The captain nodded his head. "Yes, of course. You know he gave us some vital information regarding the Taiwanese kid."

"Was Seth ever told that Quinn did not die in the fire?" Sax felt foolish asking the captain something she could have easily talked to Seth about. But, then again, he left town, and she no longer had his cell phone number.

"I had an officer call him. A voicemail was left, I believe," the captain shared with her.

"Okay," Sax replied, and then paused for awhile. "Would it be out of line for me to ask you to share his number with me?"

"Of course not, I'll be right back." The captain left his office then, and Sax sat there with her ballet flats on that ugly red carpet, wondering what in the world she would say to Seth if she called him up. She was confused by his actions while he was in Salem, he seemed regretful and maybe even interested in her again. She brushed him off, she knew, but she still found it odd that he left town without even a goodbye. Especially if he knew Quinn was alive.

When the captain returned with a phone number scribbled on a small, yellow post-it note, he handed it to Sax. "Thank you," she said, still contemplating her actions. She had his number now, but that didn't mean she would call him.

When Sax left the police station, a rookie police officer was happy he could help the captain find that phone number. He was the one who left the voicemail message the day following the fire at the old mansion. He was elated to relay the captain's message to a man named Seth Moss. The only awful thing about his simple job that day was the rookie officer had called the cell number of Jason Zimmer. Both of those phone numbers were in the same file, and a dead man had received the good-news bearing voicemail. Seth Moss still had not been aware the twelve-year-old girl had survived the fire because she had not been in that house.

Seth was sitting on one of his two black leather sofas in his penthouse apartment. He had been at Gilt Bar most of the night, drinking one Effen Black Cherry Vodka after another. He brought a woman home with him. She had been flirting with him all night. He preferred to drink alone in the weeks that he had been back in Chicago, but this woman pushed for his attention. His hands were on her now, underneath her short black skirt. He was pulling her panties off with two fingers as she went to straddle his lap. She undid his belt buckle and then opened the button fly on his jeans. His manhood was hard, erect and ready for her. At least, he looked ready. The woman positioned herself on his lap to take him inside of her, and that's when he looked up at her face. Her face. She was a stranger. Just another woman he would have sex with and then never want to see again. He could feel her hand on his manhood, but he stopped her. "Just go," he said, in no uncertain terms, and he moved her off of his lap.

"Baby, not before I show you a good time," the fiery red-haired young woman spoke, and still seemed certain he would want her.

"I'm done," Seth said, as he stood up, buttoned up his denim, and walked into the kitchen for more vodka.

After that woman left, Seth took an entire bottle of vodka back to the sofa with him. Sax Arynn had his heart. He couldn't even touch another woman anymore. He just wished, now more than ever, that things were different. He wanted to run to her, but he knew he couldn't. She was grieving the loss of a child now, and he was indirectly to blame. He blamed himself, day and night.

Chapter 22

Sax was alone in the lab with Rue again. She didn't look well at all, and Sax told her so. "So you're just going to let your condition deteriorate without trying to help yourself? Have you even seen a doctor?" Sax was wearing two-inch black heels which sounded loud on the white-tiled lab floor as she walked around a table across the room from where Rue had been sitting and working all day.

"No doctor needed when you can do your own blood testing, and when, from experience I know fatigue, weakness, and shortness of breath all mean–"

"Anemia," Sax interrupted, and Rue nodded.

"As well as a low blood-platelet count, causing easy bruising or bleeding," Rue showed Sax the back of her hand which she had bumped on the glass-topped table earlier and it had already formed a bruise on the skin.

"Thrombocytopenia," Sax added, quietly.

"Yes," Rue replied, "All are sure signs that my leukemia has come back to kill me."

"When will you tell your children and grandchildren?" Sax asked, not wanting to be angry or disappointed in her for making this choice. It was her life, and Sax understood more than anyone how sometimes you've just had enough, and there's no fight left.

"I don't want them to know," Rue stated. "I fear they will see me as a coward."

"The last thing you lack is courage, my dear," Sax said, suddenly sounding as if she was the wiser person in the room, and Rue smiled. "If there is anything I can do for you, I will. You know that, right?" Sax meant those words.

Rue nodded her head, and quietly replied, "Thank you," with tears in her eyes.

It took merely three weeks, and Rue was gone. She had not missed a day of work, although there were many days when she never moved from that stool in the lab, and Sax covered for her.

Rue never officially told Sax goodbye. It was just understood in their daily conversations which had become more open and honest between them in the last several weeks. Through her stories, Sax had gotten to know Rue as a woman. She could effortlessly imagine her as being young. She could see her with long dark hair instead of those short, loose gray curls, and with a curvy size ten figure instead of her stocky size sixteen frame which age had brought on. Rue shared so much of her life, in words, through stories stored in her memory. Talking, day after day, with Sax, had been Rue's way of letting go peacefully. Her life had been full. She looked back on her sixty-five years feeling complete. Sure, there was pain and obstacles, and even secrets. But, all of the good far out-weighed the bad, and Rue lived with not a single regret. Everything she had done, she knew, at one point, were things she wanted to do.

One by one, Rue had told each of her children goodbye, in her own way. Her thirty-four-year-old daughter, Kristie, who was married with ten and twelve-year-old sons. Her thirty-five-year-old son, Roger, who was married with fifteen-year-old twin daughters. And, forty-year-old, Liam.

She began with Liam. He was always her favorite. He was the son of the man who never left her heart, even though he never really freely gave her his. Rue's visit with her firstborn son wasn't lengthy, but their conversation over the chocolate chip cookies she had baked for him, was meaningful. They talked about him finding love again. Rue mentioned Sax, and told him, if he was patient enough, that woman would be worth his wait.

Her other son, Roger was on his way out of the house when Rue arrived. They only had a few minutes, but that time was enough to see his smile when she handed him his favorite pecan pie, and to be on the receiving end of a warm hug.

Rue had saved her visit with her daughter for last. She did so because she knew how perceptive women could be. "What's wrong, mom?" Kristie had asked, instantly observing the withdrawn look in her eyes. Her face was thinner too. She looked older, as if she had aged years in just a week or two since she saw her last. Rue had teared up and replied, "nothing I want to get into right now." And, her daughter respected that. For now. Kristie was a hairstylist and she had the day off work the following day. She planned to stop by her mother's house then. They would sit down and talk this out. Whatever it was that was plaguing her mother, there would be time to fix it.

That night, Rue Bray died in her sleep. She wasn't in unbearable pain, just discomfort. And she had prayed for God to take her.

Here she was again. Sax had pulled that same black pencil skirt out of her closet once more. She had gone six months without wearing it since Jenner's funeral. In her two and a half inch heels, her long skirt reached her ankles right where she had a tattooed chain-link anklet on her skin above her left foot. Rue's family was there, standing in a formed line of her oldest to youngest children, beginning with Liam nearest to the casket.

Sax despised this scene. She always had flashbacks of her parents the moment she stepped foot into the funeral parlor. That strange, sterile scent. The stiff, hardback furniture. Today, she couldn't stop seeing Jenner. Lying there. The images of herself having to say goodbye. And now it was Rue placed in that casket pushed up against the far wall. It was a frozen, at rest, lifeless face. Expressionless, too, and Rue had never been expressionless. Her face, with those wrinkled lines, told her story in years. Those lips had never stopped moving. She was silenced now, and Sax couldn't stand it. She couldn't bear to see her this way.

Her hand shook as she held a can of Diet Coke at her side. That woman, the woman Sax had worked with day after day for the past eight years, never went one of those days without drinking at least one Diet Coke. It had to be in a can, Sax smiled at the thought. No bottles. No fountain soda in Styrofoam. *Give me a can only, or I'll do without.*

Sax raised the can, level with the body inside the casket. She reached over Rue's body with it. She was wearing her white lab coat. Her children had decided on that because they knew what their mother's career as a medical technologist had meant to her. Sax's arm brushed over Rue's torso. It felt so hard. This woman who had been so round, soft, and jiggly, like Mrs. Claus, was no more. What was left of her now was this hard, outer shell.

Sax stared only a moment longer. There were people waiting in line behind her. She could feel the family's eyes on her. Liam was right there, only a few steps away. Sax reached into the casket and placed her hand over both of Rue's, folded hands. "Keep 'em in line, where you're going," Sax spoke with a half smile as one tear escaped and trickled down her cheek. She brushed it away quickly with the back of her hand and took a deep breath. And then she turned to Liam.

In her heels, Sax was taller than him. He stood there looking dapper with his jet black hair neatly combed, wearing a long-sleeved black dress shirt, black pants, and black tie dress shoes. "Hi Sax," Liam spoke first. "Thank you for coming."

Sax initiated a hug and then pulled him close. She spoke softly into his ear, "I'm so sorry. Your mother was something else." Liam laughed softly, as Sax pulled out of their embrace and continued speaking, "I mean that. She was so special." Sax had known Rue for years, but it was just in the recent months when she had truly gotten to know her.

Sax drove home after only staying at Rue's funeral wake for several minutes. She understood that it was a part of life to sometimes love and lose people. What she just didn't get was how much loss she had been expected to take. Grief, unfortunately, was such a familiar feeling to her. There was the shock and the sadness, and then the numbness. Sax found that when she felt numb, she could at least breathe. And that's how she had survived one loss after another in her life thus far.

Quinn was waiting for her at home again. "Hi kiddo," Sax said to her when she walked into the kitchen door from the garage and noticed Quinn perched on a stool at the kitchen table, doing her homework.

"Hi," Quinn responded, but never looked up.

"Lots of homework tonight?" Sax asked, hoping not. She sometimes helped her for hours. But, tonight, Sax already felt spent.

"Not really," Quinn responded, and Sax picked up on how she might want to be left alone. She preferred that sometimes. Sax was very good at reading various signs from Quinn. She had known her and been in her life for almost seven years, but even after nearly two months of living together they, at times, were still getting to know each other.

Sax started to walk away. She wanted to take off her dressy clothes and heels and slip into her gray sweatpants for the evening.

"I have to tell you something," Quinn spoke, successful at grabbing Sax's attention before she left the room.

"Okay…" Sax replied, turning around to face Quinn. She didn't feel tense or worried. Sax had felt enough shock in her life. Nothing surprised her or fazed her too much anymore.

"I ruined your couch," Quinn spoke.

"Excuse me?" Sax asked, glancing into the living room and then back and Quinn. *The sofa was still in place.*

"Mom always said how you loved your pale yellow things, especially your couch," Quinn spoke, looking as if she felt sick to her stomach. Sax wanted to smile, because of the mention of Jenner's name and how she always paid attention to detail, like the fact that pale yellow was Sax's favorite color. That was just a sweet memory now. "I've always been careful not to eat or drink anything too messy on there," Quinn said, still referring to the sofa. "I took a nap after school. I haven't felt the best today. Um, Sax, when I woke up, I had blood everywhere...I started my period." Sax watched Quinn tear up and then burst into a sob.

Sax felt terrible for her. *Welcome to womanhood. It sucks sometimes.* What she was thinking, she never said. She just quickly ended up right beside her, still perched up on high-back chair, and she pulled her into a hug. "Oh, Quinnster...it's okay. I'm here for you. I will walk you through this in any way I can. Is this your first time?" Quinn nodded her head and cried harder into Sax's sweater.

"I'm sorry, Sax," Quinn spoke again, pulling away.

"For what? The sofa? I love my pale yellow sofa, but guess what? I love you more." Quinn smiled at Sax, and Sax put both of her hands on Quinn's face. "Stains can be removed. You should know better than to think I'd get upset over something so trivial. You and I have been through crazy, and that makes us brush off the little things which only stir up some people. Right?" Quinn nodded her head. "Did you find what you need-ed in the bathroom?" Sax asked Quinn, not able to remember at the moment if she had a stash of pads on hand. And she didn't know if it was too soon to introduce Quinn to tampons. The idea of inserting something *up there* would naturally frighten any little girl. And, yes, Quinn was still *a little girl* to Sax. And, at the moment, she was cursing how rushed life had to be sometimes. *For fuck's sake. Let her be a kid for a little while longer.*

Quinn shook her head *yes.* "We may need to go shopping tonight for more," Sax suggested, and Quinn looked like she felt awkward. "I get this, okay? I was your age once too, and grossed out and scared to death when mine came. My friends and I, like most girls and women, had nicknames for our time of the month. Aunt Flo. And my pick, Rosie." Quinn smiled. "Sometimes you're going to wish Rosie or Flo, or whoever the Sam hell she is, would just take the first flight out and stay away…but keep in mind that your once-a-month visitor is just your body's way of preparing for one day when you will want to have a baby of your own. And, I hear those babies are worth it…" Sax laughed when Quinn started to smile at her.

"Do you ever wish you had one of your own?" Quinn asked her outright, and Sax sat down in a high-back chair beside her.

"You are the closest thing I have to a child of my own," Sax began. "I couldn't love you more if you were my own."

"That's not what I asked," Quinn spoke, with a serious look on her face, and suddenly she didn't look or sound twelve anymore. This symbolized one the many conversations Sax had had with Jenner.

"Of course I do," Sax replied, honestly. "I've just never met the right dude."

Quinn smiled, and asked, "What about Seth Moss?"

"What about him?" Sax asked, feeling what she always felt when she heard the mention of his name.

"Did he move back to town?" Quinn was curious. She liked him the day she met him a few months back, and it was blatantly obvious the two of them felt something for each other.

189

"I don't think so. Chicago is his home." Sax thought of cataloging his number into her cell phone contact list, but she had never attempted to reach out to him. *What would she have said?* Too much had happened between them, and going back seemed so far out of reach.

Quinn dropped the subject of Seth Moss, and finished up her homework in the kitchen while Sax went into her bedroom to change her clothes. After she had changed, she went into the master bathroom, attached to her bedroom. She bent down on her knees in her baggy gray sweatpants, and then sat down on her bottom in front of the cabinet door underneath the vanity. Her feet were bare with her toes painted dark blue. As she crisscrossed her legs, she opened the cabinet door and looked inside and found two boxes of tampons and one opened package of pads. There were only six pads left in there. She assumed Quinn had taken one out to use. Sax knew she needed to purchase more tonight, and she wanted to talk to Quinn in detail about dealing with *that bitch, Rosie* once a month. Sax smiled to herself, and then became serious as she started thinking. *Two full boxes of tampons. She hadn't bought any in a couple months. Aunt Rosie hadn't come to visit her in awhile.*

Chapter 23

Sax pushed the thought out of her mind as she had not moved from sitting on the bathroom floor, in front of the vanity. She wanted a cigarette. And maybe a drink, too. *Don't think about it. Put it out of your mind. There was no way. No way I'm pregnant.*

She thought of that night in Zane Ski's living room. That painting. Jenner. The closeness she felt just talking to him about her. They felt each other's pain and grief. They connected, emotionally. And then physically.

Sax had been repulsed afterward. She was furious with herself because she had lost control, and with Zane, of all people. Sax thought of Jenner right now, and how uncanny this was. There was absolutely no way she was carrying Zane's baby, after a one-night-stand. Just like Jenner. She shook her head a few consecutive times as if she could rattle this craziness right out of her mind. *She was not pregnant. Zane Ski was dead. Jenner was gone. All that was left on this earth of the both of them was Quinn, and Quinn was now hers to love and to raise. Sax was not meant to have a baby of her own. It just wasn't in the grand scheme for her.*

While at the drugstore, alone, a few hours later, Sax put two packages of feminine pads inside of her cart. Quinn had pretended to have more homework left to do, so she would not have to go along to the store to buy pads for the blood she was now forced to deal with. Sax understood, and assumed Quinn would be in this embarrassed stage for awhile. It was only natural.

She was alone in the aisle with the feminine products, and at the end of that aisle her eyes landed on the pregnancy test kits. *Maybe she should just buy one while she's alone?* She certainly didn't want Quinn to see that if she was along shopping next time. She picked up the first brand she saw and placed it into the cart. This would give her peace of mind. *Just pee on the stick, see that it's negative and move on.* Stress often times forced Sax to have irregular periods, and she was sure this was the case, again. She was frazzled in recent months with Seth's unexpected return. Then, she went through so many awful emotions the night of the fire, and following. And Rue's sudden illness had affected her greatly before she lost her, too.

Before Quinn went to bed that night, Sax sat down with her and attempted to talk her through what she could expect from dealing with the bleeding the next few days. She told her that if and when she is ready to try using tampons, she wanted her to come to her first. Or, at least Google the information if she was uncomfortable. Quinn agreed, but looked relieved when Sax stopped talking about it.

Sax was not Quinn's biological mother, but she certainly felt the angst that went along with raising a girl at this age. Sax laid in her own bed, thinking. After a few minutes, she got up, went into her bathroom, and closed the door. She locked it, too. Just in case.

She read the directions and set the stick in the sink afterward. Sax spent the next thirty minutes lying in bed, staring at the bathroom door. She had closed it as a way of shutting out what could be happening in there. *She could have two lines. She could be pregnant.* She laid flat on her back and placed her hand on her bare tummy. She was laying there, wearing only black boyshorts and a white t-shirt with no bra. Her stomach and abdomen felt flat, and fit. She was all muscle. She rarely missed a day working out with her trainer. She smoked, too. And, she's had some alcohol intake. Sax suddenly felt mildly alarmed. She could be, she calculated, three months pregnant.

Her bare feet were now on the hardwood floor just below her bed. She had only placed her feet there initially, and still had been sitting up on the bed. *One step at a time. That's how I will deal with this. If it's positive. If I am pregnant.* Literally, she walked one slow step at a time until she reached the bathroom door. She could feel her heart beating rapidly inside of her chest. And then she just turned the knob, practically marched into the bathroom, up to the sink, and saw two pink lines.

Sax wanted a cigarette so badly. She wanted to go outside in the cold air and drag on that nicotine and just forget how, so suddenly, her life had changed. Yet again. She was going to have a baby. The father was dead. She would be a single mother to not only Quinn, but to a brand new baby as well. *Her baby. This was her baby.*

Sax left work early the following day. She called her gynecologist, explained how she had just discovered that she was three months pregnant. She was worried about the baby. She was also feeling irritable, not having smoked a cigarette since the day before. The mood at work had been solemn all day as everyone was talking about and missing Rue. Sax chose to keep to herself. It was difficult to be at the hospital, in the lab, in Rue's office, without her. Sax couldn't focus on anything, and her mind kept going back to being pregnant.

Her doctor confirmed that she was thirteen weeks along, already past the first trimester of her pregnancy, and into the second. Sax was upfront. She told the doctor she had a one-night-stand, and the father had recently died in a fire. She admitted she smoked and had drank alcohol, but only wine, in the past few months. Sax listened intently as her doctor voiced her concern about Sax's smoking. The doctor told Sax in no uncertain terms, if her health hasn't been enough to make her quit smoking, then the health of her baby now should be.

Sax learned that nicotine affects the baby's health before, during, and after it is born. The nicotine, carbon monoxide, and numerous other poisons inhaled from a cigarette are carried through a mother's bloodstream and go directly to the baby.

The doctor warned Sax to quit smoking now or she would be at risk to lowering the amount of oxygen available to her growing baby, increasing her baby's heart rate, and risking respiratory problems.

Sax felt panicked when her doctor told her how there was no safe level of smoking while pregnant. It didn't matter what it took, Sax was done smoking. She had to be. She wanted to protect this life growing inside of her. She already felt connected to her baby.

Quinn was the most important person in Sax's life. She had to tell her. They lived together. She would see the prenatal vitamins, notice Sax was no longer smoking, and her belly would inevitably soon be starting to grow.

It was late, almost Quinn's bedtime on a school night, when Sax walked into the living room and sat down on the end of the pale yellow couch where Quinn was lying all covered up with the white afghan as she watched a movie on TV. "Can we talk?" Sax asked her, and Quinn looked away from the TV and said, *yes,* with sleepy eyes.

"I want open communication with you," Sax told her, and Quinn nodded her head, knowing she had nothing to hide. "I found out something today, and you need to know."

"Oh my God, Sax, are you sick?" Quinn asked her abruptly, feeling panicked that she could lose her too. Sax was all she had left, and Quinn had noticed she looked pale lately.

"No, honey, no. Nothing like that," Sax reassured her. "I'm not sure how to start telling you this, though." Sax sighed and began again. "How educated are you on sex?" Sax asked, and Quinn's eyes widened.

"So my mom never told you the story?" Quinn asked, and Sax looked puzzled. "My friend, Emily was looking for leaves in the Nature Park on the north side of town. Her brother needed specific kinds for a school project. So Emily went one way, and her mom and brother went another. There was a green park bench, deep inside the woods," Sax nodded her head, remembering seeing that bench before when she'd gone for a run on the Nature Park trail. "Two high school students were naked on that bench, and doing it…" Quinn didn't look embarrassed, but she wished her mother had already told Sax this story.

"Oh my God!" Sax replied."So then Emily shared the details of her Sex Ed, live from Nature Park, with you?"

Quinn smiled. "Pretty much. She got over it pretty quickly. She just said it looked like they were playing leap frog, naked." Sax laughed out loud and Quinn joined her.

"So you know how babies are made, then," Sax spoke, trying to find her serious demeanor again. Quinn nodded her head, yes. "I'm just going to come right out and say this. You know me, you know I'm direct. I had unprotected sex a few months ago and I'm pregnant." Quinn's eyes widened and Sax just sat there, and waited for her to say something.

"You're having a baby?" Quinn sat up quickly beside Sax on the sofa and almost sounded excited, and then Sax was sure she was. "Are you serious? Do you know how many times I've asked my mom for a little brother or sister?"

"So you're happy about this?" Sax asked, feeling like this was just what she needed. Someone else being excited about this life growing inside of her was going to help her in endless ways.

"I am, but… who's the father?" Quinn asked, as if she had every right to know. And, maybe, she did. But Sax didn't want her to know. Not yet.

Sax was quiet for a moment. "It's Seth Moss, isn't it?" Quinn asked, believing so, and Sax found herself wishing that could be true. Her silence convinced Quinn that it was. "It was so obvious that day, when he was here, how you two feel about each other."

"Quinn," Sax spoke, wanting to tell her this isn't junior high. *This is real life with real feelings and sometimes people get hurt, hurt each other, and can never go back.* "My baby's father will not be in our lives. It happened, it's over. I cannot tell you how happy it makes me to know you are excited about this change in our lives. It's another sudden, shocking change, I know, but we will survive. You and I are a family now, and we're about to get an addition."

"I love you, Sax. I love you for wanting me in your life, and now for giving me a little brother or sister." Quinn had spoken from her heart and Sax thought she had sounded so much older than twelve years old.

"I love you, more, Quinnster."

When Sax went into the shower, Quinn couldn't sleep. The baby was all she could think about. She owed so much to Sax, and she wanted help her find her way back to her baby's father. Sax had been adamant about the baby's father not being a part of the baby's life, or hers. Quinn thought of a way to try to change that.

Quinn could hear the shower water still running as she went into Sax's bedroom. She found Sax's cell phone, already charging on the nightstand beside her bed. She hurried to scroll through her list of contacts. And, sure enough, Seth Moss' number was in there. Quinn took a screen shot of his number with her own phone. And then she went back into her bedroom and closed the door. Sax thought Quinn had gone to sleep, but she couldn't rest until she made one phone call.

Chapter 24

The phone was ringing as Quinn held hers up to her ear. She was thinking of her mother, and how she always wanted Sax to find happiness. Jenner wished for Sax's happiness above her own. She used to say she didn't need a man to complete her, but Sax did. She had found her soul mate in Seth Moss, and Jenner had always believed one day there would be a chance for them again. Quinn was going to give that chance a nudge, *or maybe even a shove with news like this,* in the right direction, right now.

At ten-forty-five, Seth was asleep. He had been having trouble sleeping at night, his mind never stopped. But, tonight, he had fallen asleep forty-five minutes ago without fail.

After three rings, he finally heard his phone on the nightstand beside him, and he jolted awake. "Hello?" he said, after not recognizing the number on the screen.

Quinn realized she had woke him. The sound of his voice was hoarse and disoriented. She felt nervous about talking into the phone as she heard Seth say *hello* again. He was almost about to end the call and go back to sleep when he heard a voice on the other end. "Um, is this Seth Moss?" Quinn asked, and Seth could tell this was a voice of young person. Not a child, but not a woman either.

"Yes it is," he replied, sounding strong in his voice now. "Who is this?"

"Quinn Wibbs," she replied, and he couldn't think of anyone named Quinn who had crossed his path, other than the little girl who he met at Sax's house. *The child who died in the fire.* His mind was all over the place as he tried to gather his thoughts and focus on who it was that was calling him. "I met you once," Quinn began again. "I am with Sax." She didn't want to say she was Sax's daughter. She didn't want to say Sax was raising her. She didn't need to be raised. She just needed to be loved, and maybe guided now and then, and Sax was doing that. It was just a lot to define, and saying she was *with Sax* just sounded cooler.

Seth heard her every word. She was *with Sax*. He was thrown and felt...*haunted*. "Look, I don't know who this is, but don't mess with me!" Seth demanded. "That little girl died in a fire." He wanted to add, *it was all he thought about, and felt pained day in and day out,* but he refrained.

"No!" Quinn spoke abruptly. "That was a mistake. I was never in the house!" Quinn could not believe he thought she had died. She thought that awful scare was put to rest and behind them after she and Sax had gone to the Salem Police Department.

"Are you serious?" Seth wanted to exclaim, *Are you fucking kidding me,* but he didn't because this girl was only twelve and he was the adult here.

"Yes," Quinn answered him. "I'm fine, I'm living with Sax. My dad died in the fire, and so did the guy who started it."

Seth paused. *Yes, the guy who started it. That son-of-a-bitch Jason Zimmer.* "I'm sorry about your father," Seth said, remembering how Sax had told him she had not really known him or been close at all, until her mother died and she was thrown into living with him.

"Thanks," Quinn said. "I hope you don't mind me calling you. Sax doesn't know that I am."

"Is she alright?" Seth asked, immediately, as he was still not believing this feeling, knowing he was speaking to Quinn.

"Yes, but she needs you." Quinn was taking a big risk calling Seth and telling him this. She prayed Sax would not be furious with her.

"How so?" Seth asked, not really even caring how or

why, but just knowing he wanted her to need him again. And he wanted to be there for her and give her whatever she needed.

"She's pregnant and I know the baby is yours," Quinn said, seeming her age. It was, partly, a bold assumption. Sax had never told her that Seth was the father of her unborn baby. She had not denied it either, though.

Seth's eyes widened in the dark as he sat in the middle of his bed, bare-chested with only a white sheet covering his red boxer shorts and his legs. *Sax was pregnant? He didn't think she was involved with anyone. He knew for certain the baby was not his.* "I see, um, I'm a little shocked here. Sorry, I don't know what to say." Seth again realized he was talking to child.

"Say you'll come back to Salem and be here for her. At least talk to her. Try to convince her that she does not have to raise this baby alone. I mean, she has me, but I know she still loves you."

"She does?" Seth asked, feeling a spark of hope ignite in his heart.

"Anyone who has eyes can see that," Quinn stated, sarcastically, and Seth chuckled. He felt more alive inside than he had in a very long time. But, that excitement began to fizzle as he bluntly reminded himself that *the baby Sax was carrying was not his.*

"So there's s no man in Sax's life?" Seth wanted clarification and Quinn felt a little bit confused.

"No, she said it was a one-night-stand and the father would not be a part of her baby's life or hers." Quinn didn't want to hurt Seth's feelings by sharing that comment, which she believed was about him. "That's why I called. I want you to know she needs you."

"I will come to Salem," Seth replied, because he knew that was what this sweet, seemingly so unselfish girl on the other end of the phone wanted to hear right now. And, he wanted to know, for himself, and directly from Sax, what her story really was.

✶ ✶ ✶

Three days passed, and Seth finally stopped contemplating his next move. Of all people, he thought of Jason Zimmer and something he had said to him, prior to their trip to Salem. They had been talking about regret. *It's a waste of time and good energy,* Zimmer had said to him. *Make a change if you can. If not, let it be.*

Seth wasn't so sure his trip to Salem today would be about making a change. But, he was certain he had to see Sax again. When he left last time, the morning after the fire, he thought he had a valid reason to run away from her. Now, by some miracle, Quinn was alive and Sax no longer had grounds to hate him. That is, if she could forgive him for giving up on them seven years ago. Seth believed in second chances, but he wasn't so convinced Sax did.

He drove directly to the hospital. It was four o'clock in the afternoon when he arrived in Salem. He parked near the lab entrance and spotted Sax's car in the lot. He remembered watching her get into that charcoal gray metallic Dodge Challenger the morning after the fire. He thought, for sure then, that would be the last time he saw her.

Seth walked into the hospital and found a waiting room full of people near the lab. He asked the volunteer at the desk if Sax Arynn was available. The elderly woman left and walked down a hallway to check for him. When she returned, she told him Sax was on break. A smoke break, he assumed, and had not even thought about the danger that could bring to her baby. He briefly reflected on the last time their paths crossed in the courtyard.

He walked outside and into the courtyard. The weather was nice, sunny and in the mid-fifties. He was wearing jeans, tennis shoes, and a navy blue t-shirt. He spotted her right away, sitting on a bench. She was wearing her white lab coat, and looking chic as always. Seth wondered if her pregnancy was obvious yet.

She seemed lost in thought and unbeknownst of Seth walking through the courtyard and toward her. As he got closer, she heard his footsteps. When she looked up, she couldn't believe her eyes, once again. Nor the feeling that circulated throughout her body each time she saw him.

"Hi again," Seth said, stopping about fifteen feet from her.

She smirked first, and then spoke. "What brings you back to town? Please don't tell me you've brought in another gunshot victim."

Seth chuckled. "No, not this time. I came here to talk to you."

"You drove hundreds of miles from Chicago just to talk to me?" Sax wasn't buying it.

"I left the morning after the fire, without saying goodbye," he spoke, softly.

"Yes, you did," Sax replied.

"I never knew she survived," he added.

"What? Quinn?" *Oh dear God!* "I thought the police told you?" Sax felt terrible for him. She still remembered what it felt like to find Quinn on her couch that morning. *To find her alive.*

"No," Seth replied, "I actually just found out a few days ago that she didn't-" He couldn't even say the word *die*. What he thought had happened to Quinn, in that house that went up in flames, nearly killed his spirit.

"I'm sorry, I had no contact information for you," Sax said, realizing she had his number now and had not built up the courage to call him. Since she discovered she was pregnant, she knew that would be a deal breaker for any man. And, she cared about Seth too much to ever expect that of him. This baby was not a mistake in Sax's eyes, but she did realize, admit, and accept that her carelessness led to the conception.

Seth wondered then, and he had not thought about it before, how Quinn was able to get ahold of his number. He nodded his head, and the two of them were both silent for a minute.

"How did you find out about Quinn, if the police never called?" Sax asked him, and when she met her eyes with his, she knew she could always expect honesty from this man. She believed he was honest time and again when they were together and he told her he loved her. She knew also how badly his honestly hurt when he said he wanted out.

"Quinn called me," he answered her.

"What?" Sax didn't understand. "My Quinn?"

Seth nodded his head. "She seems to think you need my help," he began.

Sax tried to cover her nervousness that had just surfaced. She brushed back the hair covering her right eye. "What could I possibly need your help with?" she held her breath. She hoped, and prayed, that Quinn had not told him about the baby. She was kicking herself now for not being honest with Quinn. Maybe she had a right to know that her father was also this baby's father. This baby would be her half sibling. Sax's blood and Quinn's blood would be a part of this baby. That thought actually warmed Sax's heart. The irony of life was ridiculously amazing sometimes.

"I realize she's only twelve, but she really is wise beyond her years," Seth said. "She has more courage than you or I. We both could have reached out to each other after the fire. But, we didn't. We're the adults here and Quinn is outshining us with maturity."

"Why do you say that?" Sax asked him, feeling confused. *What had Quinn said to him?*

"She thinks you're pregnant with my baby..." Seth's words should not have shocked Sax. But, they did.

"That's absurd!" Sax responded, feeling like she could have gotten up off of that bench and just ran. She did not want to face this with Seth. Her pregnancy was really none of his concern.

"Well I know that part is absurd, the part where your baby could be mine," Seth told her, "but what about the pregnancy? Are you?" He watched her face, her eyes. He, too, knew he could count on honesty from her. When the game was this serious, she had to be.

"No!" she replied, feeling irked at how he had forced this out of her, and then it hit her that she had lied. She lied about the life growing inside of her that she truly did love, and want. "I mean, yes," she recanted, and Seth only looked at her while she began to explain. "I was telling you the truth when I told you I was not in a relationship with a man. I've had sex," she added, and he tried not to imagine it. He, too, had lived that kind of no-strings-attached life in Chicago, so he wasn't judging her by any means. "This baby is the result of a one-night-stand."

"Are you going to tell the father?" Seth asked, remembering Quinn's words and how she told him Sax had said this baby would not have a father in its life.

"I can't," Sax replied.

"He has a right to know, I would want to know," Seth said.

"This isn't about you," Sax all but snapped at him.

"No, but it could be," he responded, and Sax didn't know how to read his comment.

"You don't understand," she told him.

"Try me," he said, sitting down beside her on the bench.

"I only intended to come out here for a few minutes, I need to get back to work," she said, without moving.

"What you need is to talk to me. Tell me what you're thinking and how you're feeling. I'm not going back to Chicago until you do." Seth meant those words, and Sax was ultimately touched, but didn't let it show.

"You weren't worried about how I felt when you walked out on me. All those texts you ignored from me. It's a wonder I even give you the time of day now, Moss." Sax said, wanting to be angry, but she just wasn't anymore. This life growing inside of her, this blessing which had scared her so much at first, had already changed her and calmed her for what lies ahead. If she had Quinn, and now her baby, Sax truly felt like she could have a very good life. She felt complete, for the first time in a very long time.

"You're right, but I left that asshole back in Chicago," he smirked.

"Good," she added, trying not to smile.

Chapter 25

Sax opened her front door and Seth was standing on her front porch. She had just opened the door to see Quinn out as Emily and her mother picked her up for a sleepover. Sax had only met Emily's mother a few times, but she had already really liked her. She was the type of person who would do anything for anyone, and always had a kind word to say about everyone. Sax knew Jenner had loved her, and Sax hoped one day they would be friends, as well.

"Come in," Sax said to him. His visit was not unexpected this time. This time, she had told him to stop by. She wanted to talk to him in private. She was prepared to confide in him about everything.

Seth walked inside and sat down on the pale yellow sofa, and then Sax sat down there, too. Along with her sweatpants, she was wearing a long sleeved black t-shirt. That t-shirt, which was fitted to begin with, was now getting a little too snug. Seth had noticed a little belly pooch on her when she opened the door. He smiled to himself.

"I've rehashed what you said to me," Sax began, "and I want to tell you the truth. Just don't judge me when I do."

"Sax, really? We've both made mistakes. I haven't actually been living a life of celibacy in Chicago." Seth wanted to add how he only wanted her now, but he didn't.

"Okay," she said, still feeling somewhat ashamed of her actions. She had not even liked Zane Ski, and yet *that* happened between them.

"You're aware of the artist, Zane Ski, being Quinn's father," Sax began with the basic truth, and Seth nodded his head. "He and my best friend, Jenner, had a one-night-stand after meeting in a museum years ago. Zane was not at all Jenner's type. Long story short, she kept him out of her daughter's life. She eventually had to get a restraining order against him. He managed to still keep tabs on her, probably involved a private investigator or something, and he swooped in when she died and exercised his rights as a father." Sax still despised that story. She had days where she wondered if Quinn would have to wait until she was eighteen years old before she could leave and never look back, if that's what she chose to do. "I'm not sorry he died. Isn't that terrible?" Sax asked Seth.

"No, not really," Seth defended her, and meant it. "If the man was scum, it's only natural for you to want him out of Quinn's life."

"I tried so many times to reach him, to get him to work with me and allow me partial custody of Quinn. She hated it there. She and Zane were not close. Not at all," Sax paused, before she led into her encounter with Zane. "I ended up in his studio one time, at the house he lived in on Broadway, before he bought the old mansion. I was taken by this one painting of his. It was of Jenner." Seth recognized the pain in her eyes. He wished he could have met Jenner. She obviously had captured part of Sax's heart.

"I saw that painting again in the living room of the mansion. I can't explain it, but looking at it took me some place else. Zane, too. He had been in love with Jenner and rejected by her. I think his painting depicted that so precisely. We got to talking, and Zane was not easy for me to talk to. Still, we connected. He really did love her. And so did I."

Seth had a feeling he knew where this was going, but he kept silent. "He kissed me. I responded. Literally, less than five minutes later, we were naked on his living room floor. I had sex with him." Sax looked like she felt sick to her stomach, and Seth put his hand on top of hers. She allowed him to. She liked how it felt again.

"And he's the father of your baby..." Seth concluded.

"Yes," Sax said, beginning to cry. She was emotional from the pregnancy and still so regretful of her actions. But, not the consequence. "Please know, I want this baby. I'm looking at it as this life inside of me is a part of Quinn. Her half sibling."

"I understand," Seth said, smiling at Sax. She was a remarkable woman. "Maybe you should tell her that?"

"I can't," Sax said, and she was certain of that. "Maybe someday, but not now."

"She thinks I'm the father," Seth reminded Sax.

"Yeah…" Sax said, feeling like that wasn't such a bad thing for Quinn to believe.

"How disappointed will she be in me when I return to Chicago?" Seth asked. "She's going to think I abandoned my baby, and you."

"I'm not yours to abandon anymore, and neither is this baby," Sax said, feeling as if this idea in his head would never work.

"You're right," Seth told her, "but no one has to know that, except for you and me."

"I can handle my life," Sax said, feeling like he was seeing her as needy. Needing him.

"I have no doubt," he replied, smiling and inching his way toward her. She never moved, she was afraid to. She was terrified to stop him and cease this feeling of wanting him again. He met his lips with hers softly, tenderly, and then more aggressively as they seized a passion between them that had never truly gone away. Despite all of the time that had passed and the distance between them, the two of them were linked.

She had her hands on his broad, tight chest. It still felt the same. He was still so familiar to her. He reached up underneath her shirt, and she expected him to touch her breasts. She wanted to feel his hands there, and his mouth there. No matter what tomorrow did or did not bring for them, she wanted tonight to be about them again. She wanted to be intimate with him. He never touched her chest. His hand stopped right underneath her navel. He placed his open palm there and held it. Sax's eyes immediately filled with tears. Tears that wanted no part of being held back. Tears that started to freefall from her eyes. "I want to love your baby as much as I love you," he spoke those words and Sax cried harder. Seth wiped her tears away with both of his hands, and then he held her face. "Please let me."

"If this is only your way of trying to get me into bed, I swear I'll kill you," Sax responded and Seth laughed out loud. That was the Sax he knew and loved. She was tough, she sometimes talked overconfidently, but really, inside, she had the softest heart of anyone he had ever known.

"At least I'll die a happy man," he stated. "Loving you, and knowing you just might want me again, fulfills me. I meant that, Sax. I love you so much."

"I've never stopped loving you," she said, crying again. "I tried, oh believe me, I tried. But, I couldn't get you out of my heart." Seth leaned in and kissed her full on the mouth. She responded again, and they both knew it was time.

They walked into her bedroom, kissing and touching each other along the way. She laid down on top of her white duvet and Seth removed her baggy, gray pants. He threw them crazily across the room and she laughed. She had on her comfortable black boyshorts with a sports bra to match. Her shirt was now on the floor, near her pants. Seth was moving on top of her when she reached into his jeans and touched him. He wanted to savor every second of this with her. This was a second chance with a woman he knew he would forever feel linked to. But, he had come so close to giving up hope that they would ever be together again. She helped him out of his jeans and his shirt, quickly. His manhood was coming out of his navy blue boxer briefs. Sax kept touching him, exciting him further. He moved his hands underneath her sports bra and then lifted it up over her head. He touched her, kissed her, felt his chest meshed against hers. She removed his underwear with her toes and she giggled as he came down on her, between her legs with his mouth, his tongue. She arched her back, moaned his name. *God, it felt so good to say his name like that again.* He continued, he loved making her feel this way. She was the woman he loved, and he wanted to make love to her for the rest of his life. She came with a rush of emotion that momentarily left her spent. And then she felt him enter her. He was slow, and careful, at first. He had never made love to a pregnant woman before. He wondered if it was safe, and Sax assured him when she flipped him onto his back and sat down on him. She was in control as she rocked over him, at first slowly and then harder. Her hair was completely over her right eye. His hands were on her breasts and in the moment before he came inside of her, he cried out her name. The way it felt to say it, during this most intimate moment, brought tears to his eyes. And Sax was already crying.

Chapter 26

It was a dream come true that quickly turned into a nightmare. Lying there, in Seth's arms, following the most magical love making between them, Sax started to cramp. She folded her body at the middle and held her abdomen with both of her hands. "Oh my God!"

"What's wrong?" Seth asked, sitting up abruptly as the white bed sheet fell to his waist, and he feared he already knew. "The baby?"

"Oh, please, no!" Sax begged, but she wasn't speaking to Seth. She was speaking to a God she had been so distant from all her life. There was too much loss. She had never put her faith in God. Until now. This baby was a blessing, growing inside of her for months now. And she didn't want to lose it.

The severe abdominal pain continued to escalate, and Seth was scared. "We need to call an ambulance!" He didn't want anything to happen to Sax. He had just found his way back to her again, and while they had not talked about having a future together, it just felt certain.

"No, please, just drive me," Sax said, clenching her teeth and wincing from the pain. Within a few minutes, Seth had thrown his clothes on and quickly helped Sax back into hers. He never told her, but when he slipped the black boyshorts on her, he saw blood. Seth wasn't a medicine man, nor was he educated on women's feminine issues, but he feared Sax was going to miscarry her baby.

He carried her into the emergency room, just as he had Zimmer. His feelings were familiar. Panic, worry, and fear. With Zimmer, he knew he was bringing him somewhere to be taken care of. He put his trust into the doctors to help him. *Remove the bullet. Stitch him up. Send him home. Good as new.* But, with Sax, a life would be lost. If she had miscarried her baby, she would be consumed with more grief in her life. Seth felt angry. *It just was not fair.*

Seth was asked to leave and he left a crying Sax on a stretcher with tears in his own eyes. "I will be right outside this damn door!" he raised his voice, wanting to turn around and beg, or demand, for the nurses and the doctor in the ER to let him stay. *Allow him to be with Sax when she was told that her baby was gone.*

While Seth was pacing the hospital floor, just outside of the ER, Sax was listening to the doctor after he had examined her.

Her cervix was dilated, there was excessive bleeding, and she was going to miscarry her baby. Sax wanted to know why. She suppressed her pain and held her tears, and continued to ask questions. She had not known she was pregnant for the entire first trimester and just a week into the second trimester. She was three months along, at exactly thirteen weeks, and had smoked regularly and consumed occasional alcohol. She also just had sex tonight before she began cramping, severely, and then bleeding. Sax told the doctor everything she could think of. She wanted to know. She needed to know. What was to blame? *Besides herself.*

The male doctor, who Sax knew of as Jack, because he worked right there in the same hospital as she did, was sympathetic as he responded to all of her questions. He told Sax that women who smoke have twice the rate of miscarriage as nonsmokers. He also explained how drinking more than two alcoholic beverages a day can be associated with miscarriage. He assured her that sex did not bring on the dilation of the cervix, nor the bleeding. Sax stared at Jack's full head of white hair. He was in his early sixties and still thriving in his career as a physician. She was trying not to fall apart as she forced her mind on other things, like his hair and how he had aged gracefully thus far. This was just too much. Too painful to fathom. "Sax, I'm sorry, but with the contractions you are having, you are going to have to deliver this baby." Dr. Jack's words were clear to her, but she didn't respond. She just closed her eyes and the tears slowly seeped from them.

When she opened her eyes, she thought she was alone in that room which had just been in a full state of emergency. Dr. Jack had been talking to her, three nurses had been in the room, two at her side. But, they were gone now. It was quiet, and so bright in there. Sax looked over at the door. She wanted someone to send in Seth. She needed him, and he had gone from being angry to looking so forlorn when he had to leave the room, and her. Sax focused on what she was seeing, near the wall, by the door. Again, it was terribly bright in there and difficult to make anything out. White walls, floor, ceiling. She never remembered that hospital being as so. And then she saw her.

Jenner was standing there. She was wearing all white, in an almost robe-like dress. Her long, straight blonde hair, was so beautiful and shiny. Her blue eyes were brighter. Her smile was the same, so infectious, and Sax felt her heart fill up with love. So much love. For this woman, this true and dear friend, she thought she would never see again. "I don't believe this…Jenner?" Sax spoke outright. She wondered if it was really her, and then Sax thought she, too, might have crossed over to the other side.

"It's me, Sax," she heard her say. That voice. That angelic voice that truly did sound the very same way before her life ended on earth and her soul ascended to heaven. Sax may not have been a big believer in having faith in a God who pushed and pulled his people through pain and sorrow. And grief. But, she did believe with all of her heart that Jenner was in heaven.

"Oh my goodness…" Sax said, feeling like she could have cried but she felt entirely too happy right now. She was beaming. "Come here!" Sax spoke, demanding to see her up close, to touch her, to hold her.

Jenner never moved from where Sax could see her standing. The brightness in the room faded a little and Sax could now see more of Jenner without feeling the need to squint her eyes to contain a better focus. Jenner's arms were folded in front of her, and she was holding something. Sax felt her own heart overflow with a joy she had never known when her eyes and her mind registered in unison that Jenner was cradling a baby. Sax's baby.

"Is that my? Mine? My baby?" Sax couldn't string her words together at first. This was so overwhelming. She felt a mother's unconditional love. She wanted to hold her baby.

"Yes," Jenner responded. "She is beautiful."

"A girl…" Sax responded, covering her mouth with her hand. Her ash brown hair was completely covering her right eye and she brushed it away, quickly. She wanted no obstruction. She wanted to see, and feel, and hold, and kiss *her* baby girl.

"She's perfect," Jenner spoke and Sax reached out her arms. The room started to become so much brighter again, and Sax shielded both of her eyes with both of her hands, creating a makeshift visor as if she was outside in the sunshine. "I need to see her better, and you!" Sax spoke, adamantly.

"You will," Jenner spoke. "One day. Your baby is going to stay with me now."

"No, no, no!" Sax screamed. All of the feelings of fulfillment and beauty and love were fading. Sax started to cry, and Jenner shushed her.

"Shhh...this is the way it has to be. Listen to me." Oh the times Jenner had said those words, *listen to me*. It almost made Sax smile right now. She was always the voice of reason. "You are such a blessing to *my* baby girl," Jenner spoke. "Go back to her. Love Quinn as your own, as I know you already do. You have so much living left to do. Your baby and I aren't in that plan. We will be waiting for you. Just wait until you see this place, Sax. It's paradise..."

"I want to see it, I want to go now! Take me with you, I want to go!" Sax was trying to move from the bed she was sitting upright in, but her efforts were useless.

"Quinn needs you," Jenner spoke in no uncertain terms. "And so will your family." It was just too bright. Sax had to look away, and when she did momentarily, she quickly forced herself to look back. But, it was too late. Jenner, with her baby girl in her arms, was gone. Sax wanted to feel angry and disgusted and beside herself, but she never had a chance to go there. She could see through the wall in that hospital room now. There was so much depth. Everything was white, and then she could see a blue stream in the distance. Some colorful flowers, too. All colors, even pale yellow. Pale yellow may have been dominant in that setting. It was unbelievably beautiful, and Sax wondered if that was where she was going one day. She wanted to get a better look, snapshot it in her mind, and hold it there for the rest of her life. And, then, a glimpse of the rest of her life appeared on that wall. Sax saw who she initially thought was Jenner, a younger version of Jenner. But, then she realized it was Quinn. She looked so mature, so beautiful. A little girl who had grown into becoming a striking young woman. Her long blonde hair, bright blue eyes. What a comfort it was to see so much of Jenner in her.

Then, Sax could see Seth. It was just the back of him, she couldn't even make out what he was wearing. She just focused on when he turned around. She had been running up behind him. She could see herself now. She looked happy. She could feel that happiness right now. Seth was with her. They were going to make it, together. And then that feeling of fulfillment returned and Sax felt as if her heart would burst. There was a little boy in his arms. He had ash brown hair, just like his mommy and daddy. He was a toddler, maybe two years old, and he was smiling and pointing at the baby girl in Seth's other arm.

This was a glimpse of her family. A family she would one day call her own. All she had to do, Sax knew, was open her eyes.

Chapter 27

When Sax opened her eyes, that emergency room was full of those same three nurses and Dr. Jack again. They were asking her to push. And, holding her hand, was Seth. He was there by her side, and he looked strong, but sad. Sax was watching this scene, and herself, outside of her body. Like a movie on the big screen, it was all being played out before her. She noticed the hair covering her own right eye. It was messy and sweat-soaked as her forehead was beading with perspiration. She was struggling with the pain of childbirth, and worse, the pain of knowing the baby she would bring into this world would be lifeless.

"Stay with us, Sax," she could hear Dr. Jack, ordering her. "Come on, breathe, breathe. Push. Give it all you've got."

Then, Seth took over and began encouraging her. "I know this is awful, babe, but you have so much more living to do. You will persevere. You are Sax Arynn. You are a fighter." His words did not go unheard. Sax pushed. Hard.

But, there was no wail. No sound in that emergency room which had quickly turned into a delivery room. Or, maybe they had moved her. Sax didn't even know what had happened.

She knew what was happening now though, and as much as it killed her, she wanted to do it. She was back inside of her body, watching this scene from her own pained eyes. Dr. Jack had an extremely tiny, baby girl in the palm of his hand. Only six inches, six ounces. Still so fresh from being inside of Sax's womb. Sax just wanted to see her. Touch her. Truly feel her. How unfair that this was the first and last time.

She could hear Seth's sobs as he turned his back to her and then turned around to face her again. He wanted to share this moment with her. He wanted to be her rock, but he knew he was failing miserably. His heart was equally as broken.

This was the most heart wrenching thing she had ever been through. Sax had seen, touched, and cried over too many corpses in her life already. This was different though. While there was no life, there was this perfectly formed witness of where life once was. Her baby girl's body was so warm, so perfect, with ten tiny fingers and ten tiny toes. She had a nose, a mouth, two little eyes and ears. Sax brought her open palm, with her baby girl inside, up to her lips. She kissed her tiny forehead, nose, and lips. She breathed in the scent of this miracle, not meant to be.

Seth watched Sax, so closely, and he had never loved her more than at this moment. He held her, he touched the extremely tiny baby in her hand, and he continuously failed at trying not to weep. Sax was a pillar of strength to him, and to Dr. Jack and the nurses, all still in that room, all wearing solemn faces, wet with tears.

Sax was devastated, and felt the wave of overwhelming grief again. She had lost her baby. And still, she felt so much hope in her heart right now. She couldn't speak of it though. Not here. Not now. This baby girl, she knew, had gone on. Her life may have ended prematurely inside of Sax's womb, but her soul lived on. The baby she saw in Jenner's arms, this baby, was real. And Sax would see her, and hold her again, one day. This power that had come over her was unbelievable and unmistakable. It was faith. She was in awe of the strength she was given to move through this terrible tragedy. And Sax knew it was Jenner who saw her through.

ABOUT
THE
AUTHOR

As the years pass by, I find myself more and more grateful for all I have, what I have achieved, and especially for those who I love. It's effortless to embrace getting older when all around so many lives are cut short. Some, unexpectedly. Some, after long battles with entirely too much suffering.

All of us at some point in our lives will lose someone. Death is so final. The finality of the separation, disconnection, and severance is numbing. Until you realize what it means to be forever linked to someone who crosses over to the other side. The signs will be there. Lights will flicker. Pennies will be found. Significant scents will fill the air. They will visit you in your dreams. You will feel their presence in a room. It is undeniable. All of that will allow you to move on. To live. The only thing as special as memories is knowing a spirit never dies.

Two words from a friend of mine sparked the inspiration for this story. Forever Linked. It made sense, such perfect sense, to be told someone I had lost would be forever linked to me. And then the signs came. To be on the receiving end of an oddity that's both eerie and amazing is something I truly have no words for. I just knew I would have to write about it, have a character experience what I've experienced, and hope my readers would understand, or relate.

Forever Linked is my eighth novel. I hope you all enjoy this story as much as I do!

As always, thank you for reading!

love,

Lori Bell

Made in the USA
Charleston, SC
25 February 2016